The Kentucky Stories

JOHNS HOPKINS: POETRY AND FICTION
John T. Irwin, general editor

Joe Ashby Porter

THE KENTUCKY STORIES

THE JOHNS HOPKINS UNIVERSITY PRESS
Baltimore and London

This book has been brought to publication with the
generous assistance of the G. Harry Pouder Fund.

© 1983 by The Johns Hopkins University Press
All rights reserved
Printed in the United States of America

The Johns Hopkins University Press, Baltimore, Maryland 21218
The Johns Hopkins Press Ltd., London

Grateful acknowledgment is made to the editors of the
following publications for permission to reprint these stories:

"Bowling Green" originally appeared in *Occident* (© by The Associated Students of the
University of California) and was reprinted in *Antaeus*. "A Child of the Heart" originally
appeared in *TriQuarterly*. "The Vacation" originally appeared in *Occident* (© by the
Associated Students of the University of California) and was reprinted in *The Best
American Short Stories*. "Nadine, the Supermarket, the Story Ends" originally appeared
in *New Directions in Prose and Poetry*. "Yours" originally appeared in Antaeus.

Library of Congress Cataloging in Publication Data

Porter, Joseph Ashby, 1942-
The Kentucky stories.

(Johns Hopkins, poetry and fiction)
1. Kentucky—Fiction. I. Title. II. Series.
PS3566.06515K46   1983   813'.54   82-49067
ISBN 0-8018-3008-7

CONTENTS

FOREWORD

I DID SPEND childhood and adolescence in Kentucky, and set foot outside the state only four times I can remember, so that Kentucky was once reality itself, almost. But then during the following years, when circumstances kept me away except for the briefest visits, Kentucky became what it is in these stories, a state of mind. It is a state of listening for the grave and reedy voice that comes out of nowhere and with complete assurance begins its inexplicable tale. A number are stories of marriage in one way or another, and I have tried to let all of them be examples of irrational fidelity and love, wherever they have led me.

BOWLING GREEN

SO, YOU COME from there, did you? Maybe they told you about R.W. Pritchett—maybe he's there now, and you saw what he had on him. Well, I don't want to know anything about that fool's doings. But I can tell you this: nothing would've happened if he'd stayed there and tended his own business. This place could have gotten along without him and his red Pontiac, I daresay! Why, I'd been glad to see him gone in the beginning, and that Lois Meeker, she had stopped crying about him, at least. You know, we all thought we was lucky to get through high school, but R.W., R.W. just couldn't wait to go off to college. He always did set himself a little above people. I told him when he left he'd do best to stay away, but no, he had to come traipsing back, didn't he? Well, I'm not a bit sorry for what happened—ask me, he deserved more than he got, and then some.

I'm Lena Toombs, and don't think I don't know how I look. You can say I'm a redhead but that's about as far as you can go. I cut it close to the back of my head because it frizzes up so, and I let it bunch out on top so I can hide my razor in it. My daddy calls me "scarecrow," and people think my nose makes me look like a weasel. Why, I used to spit whenever I saw myself in a mirror, and I'm squint to boot. I'll marry me some old geezer that don't care one of these days. Meantime, homely as I am, when I'm down to the river there's always somebody or other waiting, and I've never spent much time talking about the weather either.

If you're back through there, I hope you'll tell this story and teach some of those college boys a lesson. I understand the college is real pretty, though. They have girls there too, don't they—learning to be schoolteachers and such? Maybe I'll get to see it before I'm dead and gone.

R.W. was just a kid like the rest of us when the Pritchetts first come here, even if they did have the best bottom land. He grew to be a nice-looking boy—not as handsome as Lois's brothers, but nice-looking, and congenial. When he was older, he'd meet me down on the bank now and again like the others. But even then he was beginning to get some outlandish notions, and don't think I didn't try to straighten him out. As long as I can remember I've been trying to talk some sense into people. Many's the time I've had to grit my teeth to keep from giving R.W. a good smack up side of the head. And when that damn cousin of his come here one summer talking all about Bowling Green, and R.W. brought *him* down to the river, why I laughed right in his face, I said, "I'm very sorry, but you better go on back where you come from, unless you want to just sit over there and watch R.W. and me do some country loving." "Lena, Lena," he started in, but I only laughed the more.

I don't mind telling all this, because I don't regret it. I don't do things I'll regret, not like most. When R.W. started courting Lois Meeker, and he kept on coming to see me, I didn't mind a bit, and I didn't mind telling her, either. I don't need to keep anybody's dirt for them. It was partly for his good I told her anyway—I didn't want him to turn sheepish and bad. The thing is, it didn't bother her after all, she had gotten so sick over him. There was craziness on her mother's side, and I don't think she's ever been quite right, even for a Meeker. I've had my eye on her for a long time. She ought to have known that if R.W. Pritchett was going to college, he sure didn't aim to marry the likes of her!

There's Meekers all up and down this river, as I hear. People say they come crawling up out of the mudflats at night. Lois's daddy runs the ferry. It don't make him any living to speak of, so he runs in liquor from the next county—and when they can't live on that sometimes the boys thieve. They're the lowest breed around here, but oh my they're lookers —purest black hair, big dark eyes, eylashes so long and thick it makes them look sleepy, and the whitest softest baby skin you ever saw—it reminds you of old river clay, it's always so damp and cold. It don't seem right.

Lois used to walk sort of hunched over forward. She never did curl her hair, so it hung straight down from her head and swung back and forth when she walked. It looked wild to me, but men liked it. When she was growing up she had a little more flesh on her than me—but that's not saying much, is it? She was always the opposite of me: she didn't talk much, and she didn't want to look you in the eye. She was knock-kneed, too, and she had a snub nose.

2

Like I say, R. W. took it into his head to court her. They had their own place they'd go to, up a way under the cliffs. She was practically a virgin—she'd only had to do with her brothers. Sometimes when R.W. was with her I'd hear her moaning and howling, and after he'd gone home she'd sit out on the rocks in the river by herself. I'll say this much for him: he always told her he was going away, and he never come close to talking about marrying her. It was her, with her crazy foolishness, that kept hoping against hope—she never let on, but I know she really thought she'd hold him. People always do that—they believe what they want, they say the sun's about to shine when it's getting darker every minute. I wanted then to beat her black and blue for her craziness—sitting out there on the rocks talking to herself. But it wasn't my place, and I don't know as it would have done a whole lot of good. Anyway, one fall he left out of here, like he always said he would.

He left early one morning in an old pickup, headed for Bowling Green, and I said good riddance. Lois mooned up and down the street all day. I was home—I had work to do—but I saw her out the window, hunched over and whispering and playing with her hair like that. She made me so nervous I had a chew of my daddy's old Rough Country. Well, on toward evening I saw her stand still for a while, and then she started up the road away from town. I supposed she was going up to Robbie Baird's to see about some sewing, but after a while I got to feeling funny, so I went up there myself. Robbie was just coming in from the fields, and she hadn't laid eyes on Lois. Robbie says she's never seen me so mad. I lit out as fast as I could go, and I caught up with Lois about three quarters of a mile up. She was walking fast, with her head down, and she wouldn't slow when I called her. When I got up with her I said, "Lois Meeker, you damn fool, where do you think you're going?" Of course I knew what she would say. How far is it—eighty, ninety miles? I pulled her down and beat her in the face till she was out cold.

I must have knocked some sense into her, because after that she managed to get along. She cried a good deal at first, but after a while she seemed to give up. All along I was telling her, "He's never coming back, he's never coming back," because his family had moved away after he left. Nobody here had enough money to buy the farm or even rent it, so the Pritchetts just locked up the house and left. It's the one off to the left down river. It's run down now, and the youngsters have started to break into it at night for the beds. It's an awful shame for that land to go to waste so. Of course R.W. stayed there when he come back, and he shingled the roof, but he didn't farm any. Anyhow, after all the Pritchetts was gone, Lois would go over and sit on their porch sometimes. And also, she started spending time by the river, up under the cliffs where she had used to go with R.W.

3

Well, R.W. was away for almost two years, and it seemed like he had taken the weather with him. A few weeks after he left, the hail beat down all the crops, and the next year the same thing happened. Besides that, they opened a mine up in the next county, and did something to the water so we haven't had any fish. Nobody had enough to eat, and I guess the Meekers was hurt most. Lois got almost as thin as me, and then she started to puff up and I knew she was eating an awful lot of clay.

Ever hear of river beans? Why, it's just clay done up with pork and tomato sauce. Most people eats it plain, though, when they do eat it. I eat me a little now and then, when I'm feeling particularly low. It does taste a little like beans, but more like river water. I bring a little bowl of it back to the house and eat it while it's still cold. It feels good going down, and it sits nice and heavy on the stomach. It makes you real sleepy—I usually don't get through more than a cupful or so. But it's not too good for you, and most around here don't eat much of it, except the Meekers. I guess they could live on it if they had to, being river people. Anyway like I said, Lois spent a lot of time up under the cliffs, and when I saw she was beginning to bloat out I imagined she was going there to eat clay by herself. I didn't go up there, so that I didn't find out just exactly what she was up to.

I'll tell you, though, I felt sorry for the poor thing. Seth said she wouldn't have a thing to do with him or anybody else—said she just didn't feel like it. He thought she'd got uppity from R.W., but I knew she was still grieving some. Judy Weldon that handles the mail said Lois had been sending some letters to him, but that he hadn't answered, and she'd finally stopped writing. The trouble was, she didn't have nothing to occupy herself. Me, I spend half the day housecleaning and cooking, but those Meekers is satisfied with a roof over their head. Then too, Lois wasn't the kind to do any visiting among the other women. I didn't owe her anything, but it hurt me to see her dragging herself around like that. I got her to come sit with me now and again, just to fill up some of her time.

I remember once I told her I'd heard about her letters, and I asked her what she expected. She looked real sullen, and said she didn't expect a thing. But after a while she got to looking so sad, with those big Meeker eyes, I had to come over and put my arms around her. I just said, "Don't take on, now." Then she said, "He snuck away, Lena, like some old dog that's afraid he'll get whipped. He couldn't bring himself to tell me good-bye." And then in a minute she said, "I'd rather he'd died than to have left me that way. That's all I told him, in every letter I wrote. I told him I wished he'd die for doing me that way." Still, I know she hoped he'd come back and marry her.

R.W. said he come here that summer because he wanted to be by

4

himself—here, of all places! He said he thought college was too hard for him, and maybe he wasn't meant to go there anyway, and he had to study all summer long or he'd fail it for sure. No, he couldn't stay with his family, because they would "distract" him. Well, he got a little "distracted" here, I think! I could have told him that he'd have better gone any place but here—for his own sake, not to mention anybody else's. But my advice wasn't wanted. Most people just itch to go to ruin. And if he couldn't bear to be anywhere else, I could have told him it wouldn't help any to show up with that red Pontiac, or wearing those loud argyle socks. I guess he hoped it would keep up his spirits, though—he looked tired and about five years older instead of two.

He didn't intend to see anybody, at least in the beginning. He'd even brought a bunch of canned goods so he wouldn't need to go to the store for a while. Somebody noticed the car up by the house, and called the constable to see who it was, and that's how we knew he was back. When I heard it I took out for the Meeker's fast as I could go. Seth, the oldest boy, was all sprawled out on the front porch sound asleep in the middle of the day. Sometimes I hate to see him, he's such a handsome good-for-nothing thing. Well, I knew I couldn't wake him up, so I barged right on in.

There's not much to that little old house. It's up on stilts, like the dock, out over the water beside the ferry line. There's holes in it big enough for a cat to jump through, and you have to watch your step because the floors is all damp and scummy. The parlor was empty and I could see the kitchen was too, so I banged on the bedroom door. Lois was in there, and she said, "Is that R.W.?"

"Not hardly!" I said. "Not hardly, it's not! It's just plain Lena Toombs," I said. I said, "It's just plain Lena Toombs, Lois, me that always has to tend to other people's rat-killing because they won't tend to it themselves." I was mad. I told her to come out from behind that door but she just said, "Go home, Lena. I don't want you to bother me any more." I'll tell you one thing: if she'd have come out and faced me then, I'd have done more than bother her! Lord, the thanks! I was shaking, and I had my razor out, ready to go after anybody.

I stared at that door for a while, and then I gave it a good kick, and I said, "I'll be more than relieved, Lois Meeker, to wash my hands of your foolishness. But before I go, there's one thing I have to say: you'd do best to forget R.W. Pritchett's name. He'll never do right by you. So if I was you I'd just stay in that bedroom so long as he's here." And then I marched myself straight home.

She did stay in the house at least during the daytime from then on. Maybe she thought everything would be fine if only R. W. would come to her. And then maybe she just felt like hiding. At night, of course,

5

she'd go up under the cliffs. But he didn't come looking for her there either, for the time being.

After a week or so R.W. asked me to come cook and keep house for him, since he'd found out he couldn't manage on his own. I wasn't in a mood to do him any favors, but I couldn't help feeling a little sorry for him. When he'd cock his head to the side, with the silly grin of his, I knew he was ashamed of how he'd done at college. Still, I kept tight-lipped and waited. It wasn't my place to stir up anything until I knew what was in his mind. I didn't even say anything about those loud clothes or the way he had cut his hair all short so you could see his scalp through it, and shaved off his sideburns. It was none of my concern if he wanted to look like a fool.

Every day save Sunday I'd go over there at noon and stay till five or so. I made him dinner and supper, and in between I did housecleaning or what have you, and sometimes I'd help him practice his great long lists of questions and answers. But I figured that wasn't all he wanted me for, and sure enough after a day or two he tried to get me into the bedroom. I let him know right then that if that's what he wanted he'd have to pay extra: I hadn't wasted my time pining after him. Well, he wasn't expecting that. He looked at me sort of funny, and then he shrugged and stuck his nose in a book. Then in a few minutes he put his head down on the table like he was thinking. I was going about my business, whistling and shaking my head. But I was really watching him, and do you know what?—he was sort of frowning and mouthing things to himself without making a sound—just like Lois Meeker! I remember to this day how peculiar he looked. Well, after a while he sat up, and told me to name my price; his voice was kind of husky. So after that almost every day we'd go to bed directly after dinner. He'd brought some French ticklers and such back with him, but I thought they were more trouble than they were worth, really.

One thing, though: sometimes he'd shut his eyes, and then I'd poke at him till he looked at me again. If I do it in the daylight, I want you to look me straight in the eyes. There's no getting around it: it's me, Lena Toombs.

Sometimes he just wanted to talk—in fact, I got the feeling he wanted me more for that than for anything. I ought to have charged him for talking, too, but I was curious to see what he'd say. I'd fix some lemonade and we'd sit us in the glider under the trees to the side of the house. It's pretty—you can look at the crabapple thicket across the river. I kept thinking he was going to ask me about Lois, but he never did. Maybe he wanted me to bring it up—well, like I say, I was keeping myself tight-lipped. We didn't talk about the old days either. Instead, he might tell me about college, or lots of times he'd complain about how hard it was to make a doctor (that's what he wanted to do). I'd say, "If it's that hard, you better not do it!" and he'd say, "No, Lena, no, I think I better." "Well, then," I'd say, "you better do a little more studying at it, and a little less gabbing and mooning. You need to get yourself straightened out, young man, is what I mean." He'd give a kind of a slow smile and sigh and lean back. He'd look up at the sky and he'd say, "You're right, Lena, I know you're right." Then why did he go on that way, I'd like to know? He'd make me mad and I'd say, "I never heard of anybody coming *here* to learn to doctor, anyway!"

I'll give him credit, though: he did seem to get a good batch of studying done at first. And I was pretty sure he was staying home nights. My house is that one up there, and from my bedroom window you can see all the way down the street to the river, so I'd have known if he'd have been slipping over to the Meeker's or the cliffs either. Lois must have heard through her brothers that R.W. had settled in for the summer, and that I was working for him. Everybody in town knew it, and some of them would talk about me because like I say food was scarce and R.W. and me (and my daddy of course) was the only ones that had all we wanted. Not that Lois would have been jealous, unless I mistake her. No, she wouldn't have minded if he'd have carried on with every woman in town, so long as he came back to her in the end. Or maybe in her crazy way she wanted to give up on him, but couldn't do it while he was still here.

He aimed to leave on September first. It was early in August he started to fidget and slack off in his studying. He'd just lay around the house dreaming. And then he'd be whispering things to himself, exactly like Lois. (You know, sometimes I got the feeling he was doing it to irk me into mentioning her name.) I'd clear my throat or snap my fingers and point at his books, but he didn't pay me much mind, and sometimes he'd have tears in his eyes. And then sometimes he'd race around in that red Pontiac his daddy had given him for college. It made me sick, it was such foolishness. Who did he think he was? College my foot! I told him I aimed to stop coming if he kept on, and I felt like it, I'll tell you. What did he do? He laughed at me, and said he'd have the law on me because he'd already given me my pay. He was only joking, though: I could tell he didn't much care whether I stayed or left. I cussed him out good then, I told him he'd come to naught. By the middle of August he'd stopped even pretending to study. I stayed on anyway. I had some idea of what was brewing. Of course I didn't know it would happen the way it did.

By this time it was me that had to get him into the bed instead of the other way around, but anyway I kept after him because I thought it was good for him. I guess by then I just wanted to keep him "distracted" till September. I remember it was one Thursday afternoon, and I'd had a particularly hard time getting him worked up, but we'd finally got going strong. He was laying all stretched out while I cleaned him up, when we

7

heard this soft little noise from the kitchen. It sort of went "Creak . . . creak. . . ." Both of us tiptoed in there, and it was Seth Meeker stealing food out of the frigidaire.

To this day I remember how they looked at each other—R.W. standing there naked as a jaybird, and Seth all crouched back in the corner. Seth mustn't have been at the clay like Lois—he was thin, and that soft face of his was whiter then ever. From where I stood I could see him easing his hand toward the switchblade in his pocket. Still, I didn't think he'd start anything—Meekers fights like animals when they have to, but they'll slink away if they can. Besides, R.W. must have been a good forty pounds heavier.

They looked at each other for the longest time, and then R.W. said, "I'd be happy for you to have what food you want, Seth. Now come on and have a drink old buddy." Seth started to relax a little then. He said he was obliged and for us to go on about our business. But R.W. said no, we'd all have us a drink right then. Pretty soon we was all talking and joking. R.W. said, "Seth, why don't you and Lena have a go—be my guest." It was high-handed of him, but I didn't care. R.W. came in the room with us and sat in the easy chair, laughing and yelling things out, and drinking more. Toward dark a hailstorm come up, and Seth had to leave. The two of them stood on the porch for a while, joking and slapping each other on the back. Before Seth left I heard him say, "You ain't forgot old Lois now have you, R.W.? She ain't said boo to nothing in pants since you been gone. And she's up there under the cliffs just about every night now, you hear?" He had to run for it then, because the hail had already started.

R.W. sat on the porch for a smoke, and meantime I was in the parlor practically jerking my hair out. What was I to do? But finally I said to myself that nothing aimed to happen that night anyhow because of the storm. So I sat out with R.W. for a while, and sure enough pretty soon he went in and went to sleep—I listened outside his door just to be safe. I put a washtub over my head and ran home. It had just cleared off when I woke up the next morning. That was a Friday—don't ask me if it was the thirteenth because I don't remember.

I thought I'd best be to the Pritchett house early, so I went directly after I'd cooked breakfast for my daddy, and what do you think? R.W. was already up and hard at work, studying to beat the band. It appeared to me to be a little late for that. I don't mind telling you, it didn't look like a good sign. He ate a sandwich and then went straight back to work. He hadn't said two words to me all day, and so I thought I'd talk to him at supper. I did myself proud with that supper—it was the last meal I cooked for him. I don't care much about food myself—I guess you can tell by looking, can't you! While he was eating his pie I said to him, just like that, "You mean to see her tonight?" He looked at me like he'd never seen me before. "Well, Lena," he said, "well, Lena, what's it to you?" So then I had my say.

"Never mind what it is to me," I said. "Never you mind that. Lena Toombs can take care of herself, which is what I wish other people could do, and if they could, things would be a lot easier for me. What is it to me? It's not one damn thing in the world to me, except I can't abide people making a mess of each other, I wish I could for my own sake. No sir, don't go worrying your head about Lena," I said, "no, just you keep your mouth shut and hear me out what I have to say, and what I've been expecting I'd be brought to say before I got you away from here, the more fool you for coming back anyway!

"You did wrong, R.W. Pritchett," I said, "you did wrong before you left in the first place. Oh I know you never told her you aimed to marry her, and I know you always told her you was going. But that wasn't enough—you know how she gets things into that fool Meeker head of hers. You let her hope for things! You let her when it was your place to keep her from it! And if you didn't know it then, I'm telling you now and you better listen good."

I said, "She'd just about gotten over you—it took her long enough —when you come waltzing back here. What do you suppose she thought, I'd like to know. Well, that's all water under the bridge. What you've got to do now is start taking care of what you do, for once in your life. With all your college ideas, maybe you need somebody to remind you this is a lonesome little old river town, and you don't forget about people here so easy—people sticks in your mind whether you like it or not. And we have to keep on getting by some way, even when you're up there at college, did you ever think about that? I guess you don't aim to come back here and doctor, and I guess that's why you think you can get away with anything you want, long as you're here, and then pick up and go. Well, Lena's here to tell you you can't! And you can laugh at me when you get back there, but right now you better pay close attention: if you don't aim to do right on your own steam, I swear I'll do everything in my power to make you do right. What I mean is this: if you go up there and see her tonight, you better get good and clear in your head what you aim to see her for. And if it's wrong you better keep yourself to home, young man. Because I tell you it won't do for you just to have a quick go at her for old times' sake. It wouldn't matter if it was me, but for Lois Meeker it won't do, because she don't have good sense—neither of you do. I'm going home now, and I'm leaving you to get straight about what you have to do. But it better be right, and if it's wrong, you better drive out of here tonight, without waiting for morning. That's what I've got to say."

That surprised him—I guess he'd forgotten what I could be like. He didn't laugh though. In fact he sort of frowned and looked serious. He looked me in the eye, and I didn't think I saw any of that old sheepishness. I went home and set myself down to watch.

Now there was a full moon, so I could see clear, and along toward nine o'clock there he was, crossing the street, headed up toward the cliffs. I saw him stop in the middle of the street and look at my house, like he was trying to see if I was watching. That decided me I'd best follow him. I stuck my razor back in my topknot, and set out. He was walking slow—I guess he was still studying about what he ought to do—so before he got to the cliffs I was close on him without him knowing it. He was walking along with his head down and his hands in his pockets, and every once in a while he'd shrug his shoulders and kick a rock or something. I hunt some with my daddy so I knew how to follow him real soft.

The rest of what happened is sickening. Myself, I don't even like to think about it much. Most people act like it never happened, and I don't blame them. It did happen though—there's no getting around it.

You ought to see the place to get a good picture of it. The ground slopes up from the river toward the base of the cliff. It's solid clay, so there's not much growing on it. About ten feet from the cliff it levels off, and there's a kind of a shelf back up under the overhang—you almost feel like you're in a cave.

R.W. walked out onto the claybank, where the ground starts to rise, and I crouched back in some bushes. The moon was low northwest, shining straight into that cleft. Still, from where I was you couldn't tell whether there was anybody up there or not. R.W. walked halfway up, and then he stopped. I felt like running out and grabbing him then, but I didn't. It appeared he was looking around for her, but didn't see her yet. "Hoo-oo, Lois," he said. Then I heard her voice coming from up there—it sounded kind of low and thicklike. "What's your business out here R.W. Pritchett," she said. And then I heard her say, "You better go on back to town." It sounded like she was crying or whining. But you might have known: R.W. didn't turn back, he started walking again right on up the hill.

I crept out into the open and followed him. It was awful quiet, but there was a bullfrog down in the river grass, and I'd take a step or two whenever he'd croak. But Lois must have heard R. W. coming on, because she yelled out, "What are you doing to me!" Those were the last words she ever said in her life. Lord, she was a miserable crazy thing—always was, but R.W. didn't help any.

He got up to the level ground, and he was still looking around for her, and then he walked forward toward the cliff face out of my sight. I said to myself that something awful peculiar was going on, so I run off to the side a little to get against the rock and I come up close to them that way. I didn't see her yet. He was standing there staring down toward the ground, not moving at all.

Don't ask me how I knew it, but right then and there I decided it wouldn't make him any difference if I walked right up to him, so I did. It was high time somebody did something, anyway. When I got there I saw what he was looking at, and why he hadn't seen Lois at first. Because she was down in front of him, lying in a sort of shallow grave. She had gotten so fat I might not have recognized her if I didn't know who it was, and of course R.W. only remembered her when she was thinnish. She had her mouth shut, but she kept making a coughing or a sort of little whimpering sound. And every time, all that flesh would shake like pudding. She had clay on her face and hands. She didn't even notice me peeping over the edge—she was looking straight at R.W., and tears was running down the sides of her face. I never saw such a mess in all my life.

Well, I looked at him and what do you think: He had his eyes closed, and he'd started to ease back away from the grave. Then he just turned around and went off down the hill at a fast walk. I didn't know what to do. Lois had closed her eyes too, and the tears was pouring out. She was nodding her head like she wanted to say, "I knew it, I knew it." Maybe that was what she was saying—she had started whispering like she always did. So then I ran down after R.W. "No sir!" I said, "no sir! You don't walk away like that." I whipped out my razor and held it on him. I said, "Now you march yourself right back up there, or you'll wish you had!" He looked real stupid, like he was drunk. He didn't seem to know what was happening, but I gave him a good push to get him moving, and we went back up there.

You guessed it: she had already killed herself with that awful old long switchblade of Seth's, that she had brought with her. R.W. looked at her, and his eyes got big, but he still had that fool's look on his face. And then he shut his eyes again, and he put his hands over his damn ears!

I was so mad I couldn't have told you what I'd do next. I probably should have killed him too and thrown him in there with her, but I didn't. I got him by the hair and pulled him down on his back there beside the grave and I held my razor against his neck so he couldn't move. He was just lying there and shaking all over, and he still had his eyes squinched shut. I straddled him and just looked at him for a while. A lot of things run through my head—I don't mind telling you I thought about cutting off his goddamn ears that wouldn't listen when they should. But then I thought of what to do. I reached down and got that switchblade out of her. And then I yelled at him, to make sure he heard me this time. I said, "I'm aiming to hurt you, R.W. and if you move—you feel this razor under your goddamn ear?" I tore off his shirt, and then I cut right into his chest, the way you cut something in a tree. I cut "B.G." for Bowling

11

Green, for all his foolishness. I cut it in capital letters. I had to keep mopping him up to see what I was doing. He kept yelling for me to stop. I think he must have gone sort of crazy, because he kept talking about Lois. I left him there and I went home. He must not have died from it — in the morning I saw the Pontiac was gone. He must have made it to some place up the road and got taken care of.

The next day when I went back up under the cliff with the Meeker boys to see to Lois I found out where all that clay she'd been eating had come from. Seth said, "She's done gnawed out her own grave, ain't she?" You could see the teeth marks all over the sides and bottom. It made me feel kind of funny. None of the Meekers could afford a coffin, so we just buried her right there. It didn't matter: animals can't smell things through that river clay the way they can through regular dirt.

I don't know whether R.W. went back to college and made a doctor or not, and I don't want to know. I said I don't want to hear anything about his doings. I've stopped troubling about such as Pritchetts or Meekers either. I do know he'll carry my mark for his folly on him till his dying day.

MURDER AT THE SWEET VARIETY

NEAR THE CONFLUENCE of the Ohio and Mississippi rivers is the town of Wickliffe, Kentucky, where I spent the first part of my life. I've hundreds of tales of those days, but my favorite is still this one of murder and the early talkies, and the woman I might have married.

The silents had been projected onto a bedsheet strung up in a cornfield outside town but for the talkies Rufus Niswonger who owned the projector converted a store on Dock Street into a theater. The seats were folding chairs and some pews from an abandoned church. It was Rufus's daughter Lucy that I almost married later—but I'd hardly laid eyes on her when Rufus was opening his Sweet Variety. In fact I'd just started to work for the man who would turn out to be Rufus's business rival and declared enemy, Alexander Cage.

Cage was proprietor and manager of the brothel. He was only about thirty-five but he'd already made his fortune since appearing in Wickliffe ten years before. He was small-boned and unpredictable, and people said that in a knife fight his savagery was awesome. He was reticent about his past, but he had connections to the north and the truth was probably something like the rumor that he'd been muscled out of a St. Louis criminal organization and forced to retreat to Wickliffe, bringing ideas and methods new to us.

My brother Horton and I started running errands and doing odd jobs for Cage when I was sixteen. Horton would have been fourteen. Mother hesitated before letting us work for the man but we had to eat, and the grocery she'd run since my father's death had almost no profit.

In the beginning we didn't have a clear idea of what a brothel was. Cage called it his hotel, and the women his guests. When we came to work after school they would usually be waking or breakfasting. Of course we became accustomed to them, but I still remember how surprised I was the first time I saw one of them. Cage had sent me after groceries. When I returned he had left, so I walked through the dusty nearly never-used dining room and pushed open the swinging doors into the kitchen. There stood a woman in underthings and those mules with feather puffs. She was eating a hunk of peanut brittle, and I remember splinters of the candy had fallen down her front. Red light from sunset came in the window. She said, "I hope you get your eyes full. Put those parcels down and go on out," but she moved her legs to make me look at them.

She was Bea Ella Lathrop, Cage's prima donna. Originally she had done her own soliciting, later had found herself a pimp, and then when Cage came she'd been the first to move into his hotel. At the time of my story she was in her late thirties. None of Cage's other women was past twenty-five but Bea Ella could hold her own. She covered her face with powder and paint and kept herself in good trim. She claimed to have the smallest waist in town.

This Bea Ella had an eye for young boys. She took up with Horton not long after we started working for Cage and she paid him to come to her in the afternoon when she was just waking up. Horton seemed to be Cage's favorite too, from the beginning, though I think it was me Cage expected to hand his business over to once I was groomed. But Horton knew how to charm people, and they said he was almost unbearably good-looking.

As soon as Rufus Niswonger opened the Sweet Variety he became Cage's business rival. Being on the river Wickliffe needed its share of entertainment, but not so much that a brothel and a movie house wouldn't compete. Rufus was a county court clerk so he had a little salary to string himself and Lucy (his wife was dead) along with, but it looked bad for a while until finally he hit on a strategy that turned the theater into a gold mine, and incidentally introduced me to Lucy. He pasted up announcements that people could see half a film free one Saturday night and then if they wanted to see the rest he would show the whole thing the following Wednesday.

The film Rufus had got from the distributor was the luckiest kind of accident for him. It starred Mae West, and we'd never seen or imagined anything like her. People gasped when she first came on the screen. Then for a long time everybody seemed mesmerized, and then people started chuckling when Mae West would make a joke and you could hear them say "Mmm" when she walked across a room. Then the screen went black and there was Rufus on the stage rubbing his hands and

14

telling us we could see the rest on Wednesday. Cage's business was slack that night.

On Wednesday the theater was full again, at thirty-five cents a head. Most had brought drink from the taverns. It didn't bode well for Cage, I saw. Selling tickets in the booth inside the lobby was Rufus's daughter Lucy. I asked if she was coming to see the picture show, she said she couldn't afford it, I offered to buy her a ticket and save a place and she accepted.

This time people were ready for the movie. They laughed and hooted at the jokes, stomped, clapped and whistled. I heard later that several couples had had congress on the floor between the front row of seats and the stage, but I didn't see any of that. Coming out into the street people were smiling, their eyes shone. In the lobby Rufus was counting his money. He said, "Lucy, you go on home, I'll lock up." That was how I first knew her name and that she was his daughter.

For the next five or six months Lucy and I had our romance. She was my first and at the time I supposed I was her first too. You'd think I'd have forgot her by now. She had soft skin and pretty yellowish eyes and fine hair, but what was so fetching about her was a sort of plainness—she never wore jewelry or lip rouge—a stubbornness that made my heart jump into my throat when she looked at me. When I began to realize I could do anything I wanted with her, as much and as often as I wanted, I was wild.

Rufus knew I worked for Cage so he forbade Lucy to see me, and so we met in secret—at least we believed it was secret—in the movie house. Rufus showed his films Saturday and maybe Wednesday, maybe Friday, and the rest of the time the building stood empty. We could come there unnoticed since Dock Street was deserted at night. Lucy had borrowed the key from Rufus and I'd had a duplicate made which we kept on a crosspiece behind a board fence near the theater. You had to push aside one of the loose boards to get it. Sometimes we'd stay in the lobby where we could see each other in the moonlight that came in the row of windows up next to the ceiling. It was clean and sweet with the fresh pine sawdust Rufus put on the floor every week. Sometimes we'd be inside the pitch-dark theater proper, on one of the pews.

If we hadn't had to keep secret and let on we'd stopped courting, maybe Bea Ella wouldn't have caused me such grief. I'd be working at the hotel, scrubbing the floor or whatever, and Bea Ella would come out of her room with nothing much on, smoking a cigarette. She'd ask me to have a Moxie with her and when I refused she'd sit down and talk about anything that came into her head at first, but pretty soon she'd get around to what she did with her customers, and all the time swinging her bare leg under my nose. I was shy and polite but I only seemed to make her bolder. She didn't go out often, but when she did she'd be sure to embarrass me in the street. Back at the hotel she'd do the most shocking things. Also she'd try to entice me with talk about me and Lucy.

Finally I had to speak out. I said, "I wish you'd let me be, Bea Ella!" She laughed and tried to hug up to me. I pushed her away and said that since she and Horton were courting she might have the decency to keep her mind off his brother.

Bea Ella shrugged and tossed her head and said, "I won't have you or anybody tell me right and wrong," and then she said, "Anyway, it wouldn't be the first time for you boys, would it now?" I asked what she meant and she told me. I can't remember exactly what it was she said. Somehow they were slippery ugly sentences my mind couldn't grasp, but the burden was clear: after all, I hadn't been Lucy's first young man. Horton had been romancing with her first and even for a while after I started.

I suppose Bea Ella said it partly from pique and then partly to break down my resistance by making me understand her desire. And then maybe it was partly to kill off any residue of my love for Lucy. The only thing I felt was plain hatred for Bea Ella, such hatred I slapped her. She didn't seem hurt or even very surprised though, but just waited to see what I'd do next. Then she grinned and started unbuttoning her chemise. I yelled at her—everybody in the hotel heard me—some of the women came for a look. I said, "Damn you, Bea Ella, damn you for meddling!"

It was only later that I thought about what she had said, and what it meant. Funny, I knew it must be true as soon as I thought about it. And I also knew I couldn't bring myself to have more to do with Lucy for a time. I didn't really blame her, or even Horton, for their not telling me. The feeling I had was like being sad and sick at the same time.

So I stopped courting Lucy, without explaining to her or to Horton. I simply quit calling on her and for several days I kept away from the café where she worked, too. When I went back she seemed to have got the message. She spoke in an edgy friendly way, as if she didn't want me to know she was resentful. Although I could tell something was brewing in her, nobody could have predicted what she was going to do. The first time it happened I was there in the café. Lucy had served Harper Gatton, the town constable, his pie. He'd said something funny and Lucy had laughed. Then she put her hand on her hip and said, "Why don't you come up and see me sometime?" loudly and exactly like Mae West. Lucy even moved her head like Mae West.

Everybody in the place laughed, it was such a surprise to see plain bony Lucy mimic Mae West. But when they stopped laughing, Lucy said exactly the same thing again. This time, although a few people chuckled, it got quiet pretty fast.

That's how it started, and it grew worse. Within a week it seemed Lucy was aping Mae West every minute, no matter what else she was doing. In general Wickliffe reacted the way the men in the café had done: amusement turned into puzzlement and then distaste. It would have been easier if she hadn't been quite such a good mimic. Even her walk, you could recognize it a hundred yards off. I tried to talk to her but she only said in her Mae West voice, "I think I have a prior engagement. But don't be too discouraged," and winked and strutted away. She was wearing a baggy calico dress but she walked as if she had on some evening gown with a train. You could almost see it, and yet there was that poor calico.

Rufus begged her to stop because she was shaming him, and then he insisted because she was ruining his business. After her antics people just wouldn't let loose and enjoy themselves at the Sweet Variety. So Rufus insisted and when Lucy ignored him he locked her in her room and boarded up the window. She screamed for a day or two but Rufus had told people what he aimed to do so nobody heeded her. Finally she quieted. Still people kept away from the picture show for several days, and when they did start coming back it was only a trickle. To boost business Rufus announced that a new Mae West film would open Saturday, and that there would be a door prize. There would be only one showing at ten-thirty. By then, Rufus thought, people would be drunk enough not to have any compunctions about coming.

I'd felt sorry for Lucy ever since she'd started aping Mae West. Now that Rufus had locked her up I thought maybe she'd come to her senses some, and so on Saturday afternoon, the same Saturday as Rufus's door prize showing, I walked in and up to Lucy's door and knocked. She said I couldn't stay because Rufus was coming back. She apologized for the way she'd been acting. She said she'd like to talk more, and we could meet in the lobby of the Sweet Variety at three in the morning, since Rufus aimed to unlock her that night after the show. In spite of all the other excitement I kept thinking about Lucy in the back of my mind all that night.

Apparently Cage didn't intend to let Rufus win back his business without a fight. He, Cage, had put up a notice that there would be free beer and dancing at the hotel starting at eight. I was to tend bar until eleven, and Horton would serve as cashier and usher upstairs.

I'd never seen Horton so excited. When we were getting dressed for the evening I asked him what he had on his mind, and he claimed it was the dance. After his bath he looked at himself in the mirror for a long time, and then he said, "I guess Mae West herself wouldn't object to some

17

loving from one of us handsome boys." I asked where he'd learned to talk that way and he laughed. I laughed too—I was feeling good.

The hotel party started well. People had lined up to wait for the doors to open. Most would have a glass or two of the free watered beer and then begin buying hard liquor. A number of respectable people showed up, and wives were seeing inside the hotel for the first time. Cage's own women didn't come down till people were feeling too happy to object. There was every kind of dancing, waltzes, fox trots and back country jigs all mixed together. The band was fiddles, a piano and an accordion, and one saxophone, an instrument most of us had heard only on phonograph records.

At nine-thirty during my break I went up to see how Horton was doing. He'd been drinking some and he seemed a little nervous. He asked if I'd seen Bea Ella. Nobody had seen her yet, or Cage either for that matter.

I was back at the bar when Horton took his break. He certainly looked good, especially dressed up the way he was that night. As soon as he came down people were all over him, talking to him and touching him. It was the kind of thing he loved, and he was about to let things go too far, when we heard women on the front porch and in the hallway start squealing and gasping. None of us in the ballroom could see what it was until someone yelled "Make room!" and a corridor opened in the crowd and in walked Cage and Bea Ella.

Cage was more dandified than ever, but what made the women squeal was Bea Ella wearing a stomacher that looked like it had a million rhinestones in it. We knew Cage must have given it to her since he was the only one in Wickliffe who'd ever have seen such a thing. It was sensational. People said it hurt their eyes. Horton like everybody else had turned to stare, and Cage and Bea Ella walked past him without so much as nodding. He seemed taken aback, and then the meanest look I'd ever seen came across his face, and he shrank back among the crowd. That was the last I saw of him that night. Meantime Cage and Bea Ella had made their way to the bar. I served them drinks and people started dancing again.

Cage of course hoped that ten-thirty would pass without anyone's noticing it, but people were in holiday spirits, greedy for pleasure, and most left for the Sweet Variety when it was time. If it disappointed Cage he didn't let it show. But Bea Ella who'd enjoyed all the attention now sulked. She'd drunk a good deal, and that didn't help her mood either. Finally she told Cage she was going off to the picture show too. None of Cage's women had ever stood up to him that way. He didn't say anything and she flounced and stumbled out into the street. Cage walked back to his office, thoughtful and sad.

By then it was eleven-thirty, my quitting time. I'd planned on slipping in to see the last of the new movie myself, but when I got there it looked so crowded I walked on down to the river and sat there for a while. I'd been drinking myself, and I thought the fresh air would sober me.

I thought about Lucy Niswonger locked up in her room. I thought about how kind she'd been to me, about the color of her skin and hair, and how she could sit perfectly still not doing anything. I thought how sad it was that she had been so unhappy without deserving it and I wondered what her life would be like in the future. A breeze came up, and I thought a while longer and finally I decided to ask Lucy to marry me when I saw her later that night.

Just then the doors of the movie house flung open and the crowd pushed out into the street. More and more came out. They milled around muttering and cursing, throwing ugly looks back at the theater. When some got nearer I found out what had happened. In the middle of the movie Bea Ella had arrived. She had strolled down the aisle and up onto the stage in front of the screen so that part of the moving picture fell on her with all her rhinestones. The amazing thing was that she had taken it into her head to imitate Mae West, or to imitate Lucy's imitation. People now saw that her hairdo and dress and even the stomacher had been a sort of Mae West costume. The audience had hissed and shouted and thrown whatever came to hand. Bea Ella had vanished into the wings. They'd supposed she was escaping into the street and had milled out half in pursuit of her, and half simply because they couldn't bear the film any more.

By the time I'd heard this, fights had broken out. Harper Gatton, the constable, was doing what he could to stop them, but still it looked ugly, so I got past the crowd and went on up toward the quiet square. I sat on the courthouse steps for a while. One tavern was still open on the south side, but I wanted to rest so I went home to wait till three. It must have been around one when I got there. There was light in every room. Mother often lighted the house to discourage burglars but I couldn't believe she'd be out so late. I was going up to knock on her door when she arrived, white and shaking. She said, "I've been looking all over for you. What mischief has that Cage and his crew led you into?" I was starting to explain my whereabouts when she said, "No, I won't tempt you to lie to your mother. Just lock the house and don't disturb your brother when you come up."

I sat in the kitchen and had a cup of coffee and dozed off even so. When I left the house I noticed that the town was completely quiet. I could even hear the river half a mile away clear as my own footsteps. It was quiet when I came to the theater too.

The key was gone from its hiding place, and the theater door was unlocked. There was enough moonlight for me to see that the lobby was empty. I whispered, "Lucy, Lucy!" Then I heard a noise from the ticket booth. I thought she must be hiding so I crept up and jerked open the door. On the high stool sat Bea Ella Lathrop. It took me a moment to get over the surprise, and then I said, "Where's Lucy?" She didn't answer. I guessed she was drunk so I shook her and said, "Bea Ella, what's happened to your rhinestones?" because they were gone. Then her mouth fell open and blood spilled out. It scared me so much I jumped back away from her. I had another shock when something seemed to move on the floor near Bea Ella, but then I saw it was two or three of the rhinestones dropped there, that had sparkled when I'd moved my head.

I still didn't have my wits about me when I heard the door open behind me. I thought it must be Lucy so I said, "Lucy, get away from here." But it was Harper Gatton. He held his gun on me and warned me not to move. While he examined Bea Ella as best he could in the moonlight he told me he'd been on his way home after having locked up some men for fighting, and he'd heard a scream from this part of Dock Street so he'd been checking doors and when he'd found the Sweet Variety door unlocked he'd known something was wrong. He said Bea Ella was dead. She'd been clubbed on the head and back. Gatton said he didn't think I'd done it but that he'd have to jail me for the night.

The next morning Gatton let me go. He asked me not to let anyone, not even Mother or Horton, know about Bea Ella. He said he had to investigate and it would be easier if we kept her death secret awhile. Also he said again he believed I was innocent but I shouldn't leave Wickliffe. I said Cage would have to know about Bea Ella, but he said he'd spoken to Cage during the night.

When I got home Horton was out and Mother was still asleep, she'd been up so late the night before. I made breakfast and thought over what had happened. There had been something troubling in Gatton's manner, a sort of resignation as if he believed I was innocent but expected to charge me with the murder anyway. That was why I decided I should do some investigating myself. It had come to me during the night who could have killed her, if she had been murdered, and not died by some accident.

I mentioned that before going in with Cage Bea Ella had used a pimp. His name was Smith and people called him Smitty. He was an early example of a type you can find now around any bus station, slight but proud of muscles he'd developed not by any work but by pushups, with pale skin and greasy hair, unmarried and old enough, probably thirty, for his way of life to seem pitiful. It was this Smitty I first suspected of killing Bea Ella, out of revenge for having left him and going to work for Cage, and also to get the rhinestones—Smitty was fool enough to steal

20

them without stopping to think he couldn't sell them in Wickliffe anyway. It wasn't so much that I thought he actually had killed Bea Ella as that he was the only person I could understand killing her. And if he had done it I imagined she had given him ample provocation. I planned to satisfy myself that he was guilty and find proof if I could, not for justice's sake, but so that I'd have a way of protecting myself if it came to that.

I visited the boarding house on the south side where he lived, and found him gardening for his landlady. His head was bandaged. I asked about it and he explained that the night before, drunk, he had tried to climb the Civil War statue in the square and fallen. Dr. Freeman had stumbled on him, brought him to his office and kept him there the night. When I asked about the time of his accident he said he wasn't sure but that it was early.

By then it was time for me to do some painting for Cage at his home. I found him sitting on his front porch steps in the sun, spruce and calm as ever. He looked at me in a way that reminded me of the way Harper Gatton had looked at me that morning, and before I could say anything he motioned me around to the side of the house where the ladders and paint awaited me.

All that day I'd managed to stay away from Horton, not wanting to have to lie to him, but in the evening after supper he came to my room and what do you know, he'd already heard about Bea Ella. Gatton had realized Cage's women and also Horton would have to be told. Horton was worried about me. He said it didn't make sense, but he thought Gatton really suspected I'd done it. I laughed, but he said, "No, I mean it, I think he aims to string you up." He said, "He'd never try to catch up with you if you stowed on a boat to New Orleans or St. Louis. Or you could go overland out to Kansas City." I could see Horton had given some thought to my welfare.

I hadn't forgotten Lucy. I could have cut my tongue out for calling her name that way at the theater. I hadn't had a chance to see her all day and now I began to think maybe it was a good thing: if Gatton was suspecting people as crazily as Horton seemed to think, it might incriminate Lucy if I saw her too soon. And then there was the fact that I'd have to ask why she hadn't come to the theater, and yet at the same time lie to her about what had happened there, and I knew that wouldn't be easy. I decided that when I did see her I'd postpone proposing marriage since I didn't want our engagement mixed up with Bea Ella's death.

Horton's talk also made me decide that things were more urgent than I'd supposed. I decided, in fact, that I had only about two days to find out what I could. In the hot damp weather, that was about as long as it could be kept a secret that Bea Ella was in a broom closet at the movie house, and when the secret was out it was always possible I'd be locked up and so unable to investigate. Luckily Cage had said he didn't need me for the next two days, so that my time would be my own.

So that Sunday night after Horton left me alone I sat down and wrote a list of questions, and if I could think of any answers I wrote them down too, no matter how ridiculous they seemed.

1. Did somebody kill Bea Ella? I can't say. But somebody did put her in the booth and take her stomacher.

2. Why was the theater door unlocked? Rufus might have forgotten, or maybe Lucy had already been there when I arrived.

3. Where had Bea Ella been between about 11:40 when she ran into the wings of the theater, and 3:00 when I found her? Maybe she was hiding in the theater the whole time. If not, I'd better find out where she was.

4. Can anybody swear I hadn't got there in time to kill her and put her in the booth? No, because Mother was the last one to see me, and that was only about 1:00.

5. Why might people think I'd have wanted to kill her? Because she'd been after me so, and because she'd told me bad things about Lucy, and to keep her from telling other people those things.

6. Who else might people think had a reason to want her to die? Smitty. Horton, because of how she had scorned him that night. Cage, for the same reason or some other. Lucy, because of some crazy jealousy. Rufus, because of Lucy, and because she'd spoiled his opening night. Almost anybody in the movie audience might have felt like it that night.

7. Are there any others? Maybe she'd shamed or cheated one of her customers, or maybe somebody off the river had seen her rhinestones that night and killed her to get them and was already gone.

The list helped, and yet I remember as I sat looking at it before I went to sleep I had a nagging feeling I'd left something important out. It was like my mind was trying to tell me something but I couldn't make myself hear it. Then or later I didn't consider sneaking away from Wickliffe. I must have believed that being innocent I was bound to be exonerated. Remember, I was seventeen.

Since Smitty was my prime suspect I went to check his story first on Monday morning. I should explain about Dr. Freeman. He was our family doctor, and when my father came down with pneumonia Dr. Freeman had attended him to the end. Freeman had once been a sweetheart of Mother's, and after Dad had been dead for a couple of years Mother made some feeble effort to court Freeman, partly for Horton's and my sakes, not for the money but because she said we ought to have a man's guidance. All this made it hard for me to verify Smitty's story with Freeman. I had to lie to explain my questions, and of all the people in town it would pain me most to lie to Freeman.

I told him Cage wanted to know about Smitty. It seemed the perfect pretext since Cage's wishes were notoriously unaccountable, but even so I felt Freeman's shrewd eyes searching me as I told this lie. He said he had found Smitty in the square unconscious and bleeding. He had a mild concussion and had kept losing consciousness through the night while Freeman sat with him. In any case, Freeman was certain he had found Smitty about 12:15. And I knew if there was anyone I could trust, it was Freeman.

When I left his office I wandered down to Dock Street. It occurred to me to check whether the Sweet Variety key had been returned to its hiding place. It hadn't. By then I was ready to see Lucy, finally, at the café. I sat near the back so we wouldn't be overheard. Lucy was pretty in ways she'd never been before. She was at ease and looked happy, and there wasn't a trace of the Mae West manner.

I came early so she'd have time to talk. She brought a cup of coffee for herself. She smiled and didn't say anything, so right off I asked why she hadn't come Saturday night. I was prepared for almost any answer except the one she gave me. "My gracious, I forgot," she said. "Why yes, I was going to meet you there, wasn't I." She said she was ashamed for forgetting, and said, "Well, did you go and wait for me?" I only said "Yes," and let her apologize again. She talked about this and that and then all of a sudden she said, "Oh, have you heard about Bea Ella Lathrop?"

It shocked me so that my mouth fell open, and Lucy laughed. She said, "No, not what she did at the movies. What I mean is she's gone, packed her bags and gone." I never knew who started that rumor—Cage, Gatton, maybe just townspeople who'd noticed Bea Ella's absence and had to account for it. The way I said I hadn't heard it made Lucy laugh again.

The café was filling up so she couldn't sit talking any longer. I asked what she had done with the lobby-door key. She said, "Isn't it there?" I said children must have stolen it, and let her go back to work. On my way out I patted her on the shoulder and said, "Bye, Lucy." She gave me an absent nod and smile.

That afternoon I idled around talking to people who'd been out Saturday night. The trouble was that most of them had been drunk, hectic or stupefied, and so hadn't noticed much. But none of them had seen Bea Ella for sure after she'd run off into the wings. One would say, "Wasn't she over in Strether's when we were all singing?" but then another would say, "No, the only women there were Strether's wife and daughters." It was like hunting Will o' the Wisp down through the sallows.

I did, though, discover some information I hadn't counted on. Cage, it turned out, had stayed in his office til 1:45 when the party had to be over by city ordinance, and then he'd walked home. This was attested to by

23

witnesses who'd been at the hotel dancing till closing time and some of whom had walked with Cage most of the way to his house. So he definitely could not have done the murder. From the hotel to his house took over half an hour at a brisk walk, and that night he and the others had taken their time, so that the last witness would have left him walking toward his house no earlier than 2:45 or 3:00. Cage just couldn't have got back to the theater before I arrived there.

Before he'd left the hotel, though, two interesting things had happened. First, Smitty had showed up mumbling he wanted some money. He'd barged into Cage's office. There had been an argument, Smitty shaking his finger and shouting, Cage sitting behind his desk, unmoving but clearly angry, saying little until he stood up and pushed Smitty out through the lobby and down the steps into the street. This was a little after midnight, in fact just a few minutes before Dr. Freeman had found Smitty in the square.

Later, shortly before closing, there had been a letter for Cage. No one could remember where it had appeared from—suddenly they all were yelling "Letter for Mr. Cage" and passing it around until Cage himself took it, read it, and that was that.

At supper mother seemed herself. Horton was more agitated than ever about my staying in town, though he was careful not to let Mother notice. Later he came to my room again to beg me to go. When I'd got shut of him I went out again. The taverns closed at ten on week nights so I didn't have much time. I went from place to place buying beers and coaxing people into conversation about Saturday night. But I didn't learn more than I already knew. There weren't many people out on a Monday night and most of them were off barges just tied up for the night.

When the taverns closed I walked down to the river with some of the bargemen. One in particular wasn't much older than I. He must have seen my worries on my face because he said, "I don't know what's your trouble, but listen: my uncle runs this barge, and I'll vow if you want to leave out of here before sunup with us, you're welcome." I said I guessed I wouldn't, but I thanked him for the offer. We sat on the barge talking for a while longer, and then I walked back up into town.

Everyone had gone to sleep. Dock Street looked like nobody had walked on its sidewalks in years. I passed the movie house, where Bea Ella was still in the closet. After I'd got a way beyond it, something possessed me to turn around. I stood there looking and listening. There was a full moon in a clear sky. I could hear the river gurgling, and now and again lines on boats creaked. The river reminded me of somebody breathing. I came walking back toward the theater, the way I'd done before, past those dingy storefronts and houses with half boarded-up windows all silvered in the moon, where anybody at all could have been hidden to watch me. Like I knew what to do I pulled back the fence board the way I'd done on Saturday night and reached in and around, and laid my hand on the cold metal of the lobby-door key.

I don't know why, I didn't move for a minute. I remember I felt I'd fallen into a trap, and the crazy idea flashed through my head that somebody had wired the key and I was being electrocuted, the key felt so cold, and the river air had made it sweat. I broke out in a cold sweat too and then somehow I knew there was somebody across the street behind me, somebody watching me from over there in front of the Sweet Variety, who had been standing there all along in a shadow while I'd walked up and down the street. I took my hand off the key and turned around, and saw who it was: Alexander Cage watching me with a sort of thoughtful look on his face, like he didn't care what I did, he was just curious. I walked over to him. He was rubbing his chin—he hadn't shaved since morning, and I remember I noticed how black the shadow along his jaw was, and how his diamond ring twinkled, and how thoughtful he seemed. I thought I had to say something so I said, "Evening, Mr. Cage. I was out for a walk." He didn't reply. I nodded and started home without looking back, but listening to see if he was following me. Halfway, in the square, I started to run, and then I realized that Wickliffe was so quiet Cage down on Dock Street could hear me, know I was running, and then the cold sweat came over me again and I had to vomit. I remember the moon made it look like quicksilver falling out of my mouth.

The next morning it seemed so much like a dream that right after breakfast I went down to Dock Street to make sure the key really was there. Then I came back to the courthouse where Rufus Niswonger's county court clerk office was. He was surprised to see me and couldn't decide what attitude to take. Anyway, it was a relief not to have to pretend Bea Ella had left since Gatton had told Rufus about her.

I told Rufus I hadn't killed her, and I asked if he knew how much longer it would be before Gatton told everybody. Rufus said Gatton had promised to move her before Wednesday night, when Rufus ordinarily would show a film. Then I said, "The thing I can't understand, Mr. Niswonger, is who unlocked the lobby door." I asked if there was any chance he'd left it unlocked. He said there was a chance, he was forgetful and the excitement had upset him. He said he couldn't be sure now, but he thought it was likely. I asked when he'd left. He said he'd been in the booth counting money when the trouble had broken out, and he'd been afraid of robbery so he'd stayed there till everybody had rushed out. Then he'd locked the front door and waited till the street was quiet and then waited a while longer, and then gone home around 12:45.

In the afternoon I went over to the hotel. I slipped in the back way and listened a while to be sure Cage wasn't there, and then went up to talk to one of the women, a girl named Faye who'd seemed friendly to me.

I told Faye I'd been found at the scene of the crime and might be charged. I asked if she knew who'd done it, and she said she had no idea. Somehow she seemed evasive though, so I said, "Let's talk about Bea Ella for a while, and I'll buy us a drink." She loosened up some. She said, "I don't know who did it but I expect she drove him to it, because she was turning mean in the last few months. She may have started feeling her age, but that wasn't the only reason. Your brother, yes your brother Horton, there's no excuse for the way he was treating her, and the worst of it on Friday night before the party." Apparently he'd been humiliating her before the other women and customers. Finally she'd shouted at him, told him he'd find the world didn't need to come begging to him, and stormed out. He'd laughed and said he didn't know about the world, but he was confident she for one would be back before very long. As I left, Faye said, "You've got more out of me than Harper Gatton did. He didn't have the sense to buy me a drink." It was the first time I'd crossed the trail of his investigation.

The rest of the afternoon was uneventful. I had supper in a little place on the wharf where I could mix with the boatmen. News travels fast among them, and I felt sure I'd hear of it if somebody had appeared up or down river with a hoard of rhinestones. But there was no such news. So I ate slowly and lingered over my coffee and pie, and gave my mind to thinking about the view of Horton Faye had given me. It was true he was old enough to decide things for himself, but still I began to think I'd neglected my responsibility of looking after him and giving him my best advice.

I walked back in the dusk. As I turned into my street I noticed the light in Horton's room go out. It seemed early for him to be going to sleep and something told me to wait and watch.

After several minutes, sure enough Horton came out of the house, out the side door so he wouldn't have to pass the parlor where Mother sat sewing. I stepped back between two hydrangeas and he passed without seeing me. I followed. I couldn't figure out what he was up to until I realized he was headed north, but detouring through alleys and back streets. When we came to the edge of town he kept going, and then I guessed he must be headed for Cage's. I thought of turning back, but I didn't.

Summer evenings the north road was always foggy, and that night it was especially so. The high corn seemed to hold it. Horton disappeared and since he was walking quietly, and soon I couldn't hear him either, I sat down and waited half an hour so I wouldn't catch up to him by accident.

When I came to Cage's the only lights were upstairs. I could have climbed the willow beside the house and tried to peek in a window. Instead, I crept right into the house, up the stairs toward Cage's bedroom where I could hear his voice. If he'd caught me and it had struck him the wrong way, he'd have killed me with his derringer or even his bare hands. I'd once watched him cripple a man twice his size. I thought of all that, and yet I kept on tiptoeing up the stairs.

The door was thick oak and muffled sound so I had to get up against it before I could distinguish words. I remember the next moments well. I heard Cage say, "Yes, Saturday night she was here screaming at me, accusing me." I could imagine Bea Ella bursting in, covered with the refuse the theater audience had thrown at her, furious in her liquor. It didn't occur to me yet that there hadn't been time for her to see Cage there and get back to the theater before three. It didn't occur to me because I myself didn't have time to think: Cage was saying, "I'd thought I heard a noise from the hallway. I came to the door like this and," and with that he flung open the door I was standing behind too amazed to move. He had on a silk dressing gown. Behind him near the foot of the bed stood Horton undressing. And in the bed sat Lucy, apparently naked, with the sheet held over her breasts.

Cage looked at me for a moment with raised eyebrows, and then he gave me a warm smile and clapped me on the shoulder, and said, "Welcome."

What could I do? I apologized for eavesdropping and told Horton he ought to be getting home before long. I didn't speak to Lucy. Anyway, I managed to leave. I'd been lucky Cage hadn't taken it into his head to be angry.

The next day they took Bea Ella out of the movie house. The town was full of talk, and I heard one person say, "I knew something was wrong when I saw how careful Rufus was to lock up Saturday night, how he came back white as a sheet to make sure the door was locked." Later that day Gatton arrested me, charged me with killing her, and told me he'd have to lock me up again. Everybody in town seemed to have heard the story by then. They stared and pointed as Gatton led me off to jail.

The trial was six weeks later. I didn't stay in jail all that time though. After two weeks Gatton said I could be bailed out. I'm sure Mother got the money from Cage. In the meantime Bea Ella had been buried. When I walked out of the jailhouse people still stared but they seemed friendly and even tried to engage me in chat in their awkward ways.

In those six weeks I grew up, I guess, and became a man. I don't know which taught me most, watching the townspeople's attitudes toward me or solving the murder. Soon after Mother bailed me out it all started to fit together. I might have solved it sooner but I had Lucy on my mind.

She didn't visit me in jail and so as soon as I got out I visited her. She seemed surprised and not much concerned when I reproached her. I said I'd intended to ask her to marry me, and I'd thought she had similar feelings for me. She smiled and tears came into her eyes. She said she was honored I'd thought of marrying her, but she said she wouldn't have accepted. And then she leveled with me. She'd been fond of me, but Horton had always been at the back of her mind. She said she was wild for him, she couldn't help herself. She'd aped Mae West not because I'd stopped seeing her, but rather because she seemed to have lost Horton for good to Bea Ella and Cage. I remember she said, "Those three did things you couldn't imagine, things I hardly imagine even now that I'm taking her place." She said, "You don't know your brother. He's old, older than you and still doesn't have his beard yet."

Her being flat honest like that, her looking at me with those clear amber eyes made me all of a sudden want her again the way I did at the beginning, as if not a thing had happened, and I said, "Lucy, let me see you tonight so we can talk and get things straight."

Lucy said, "It's too late. For my own good I almost wish it wasn't."

What she said helped me grow up too, especially since she was kind. I think, though, she wasn't right about Horton and me. It's true I was just starting to grow up, but Horton hadn't started and in a way he never did. He's quiet and settled now but underneath he's still a boy.

The night after the day I talked with Lucy, the day I got out of jail, since it was hot and I couldn't sleep I came down and entirely by chance brushed aside the lace curtain and found tucked back into a corner on the window ledge one of Bea Ella's rhinestones.

During those days in jail I'd been worrying about Lucy I'd almost forgotten Bea Ella, but now finding the rhinestone made me remember her, and say to myself that no matter what she'd done, she hadn't deserved to be killed that way. I thought of her in the dark theater as I imagined, drunk but sobering as she realized her danger, holding her hands up to protect her face and then stumbling away—how she'd have screamed until the blows knocked her unconscious, screamed for help. I flipped the rhinestone out the window into the darkness and sat down at the kitchen table to think. By dawn I had most of it worked out. A few details didn't make sense yet but I got them straight in the next few days.

Meanwhile during the end of July and August more of the rhinestones from the stomacher turned up. None of the townspeople told me, but without trying I noticed. Coming into the courthouse to ask Gatton if he couldn't hurry the trial I'd glimpse the sparkle in the sand of an ashtray. On the street I'd hear a child yell "I found one!" People sold them to rivermen at first but before my trial they began to keep them and to talk half-openly about them, though not in my presence. I could tell when across the café the subject had come up because it made eyes sparkle. And then during my trial the business seemed to break. There was a late hour when light came slanting in the high windows of the little courtroom. Both audience and jury would be partly shadowed so that it was impossible for me at the defendant's table to make out more than a gathering of dimmed shapes. Across it would be a play of the rhinestones people by then were openly wearing on their persons, twinkling in the sunset.

I never saw Lucy with one. I wondered if she hadn't found any, and I didn't know till Cage took her away with him almost a year after the trial. I guess Cage had decided it wasn't worth doing battle much longer with the petty businessmen and police. Or maybe he decided to go because he'd lost both me and Horton. After the trial I couldn't bring myself to work for him any longer. And with Horton too things seemed to sour. Maybe Cage had begun to demand things even Horton wouldn't or couldn't do. Anyhow Cage left one night and Lucy went with him. Rufus followed them into Tennessee and then gave up. It was characteristic of Cage that his last official act in Wickliffe was deeding the hotel and his house to Rufus. Lucy too had left a bequest, in the hands of one of Cage's women. In fact Horton and I first heard about their departure from the woman when she came with the rhinestones Lucy had left, one for Horton and one for me.

Lucy's and Cage's departure indirectly provided the link I knew must be there but had no way of discovering in my investigation of the murder. Almost immediately Smitty, the man who'd pimped for Bea Ella and whom I'd first suspected, had to be jailed for disturbing the peace at Dr. Freeman's. He'd burst in and demanded money he said Cage had given the doctor to keep for him. Freeman had denied the accusation, Smitty had refused to leave and Freeman had called the police. Gatton locked Smitty up for a week and then let him go, warning him not to make such accusations unless he had proof.

I knew Freeman wouldn't have withheld money from anyone. Smitty's claim was so bizarre from every angle that it was puzzling to wonder how it could have entered his head to make it. People laughed and said the syphilis must have caught up with him. But I guessed that Smitty's move had its own logic. Mistakenly, but with some reason, he believed Cage had given Freeman money because on the morning after the murder Smitty had recovered consciousness in Freeman's office long enough to spy Alexander Cage, of all people, in conversation with the doctor. He may not have remembered it at first when he fully regained consciousness but in time he did remember it and it puzzled him. Especially as he mulled over the events of the night of the murder and came to realize that the good and unimpeachable doctor had simply lied about the time at which he had stumbled on Smitty in the street. Smitty had guessed rightly that the doctor's lie had resulted from Cage's visit that morning.

Beyond that Smitty was in the dark. He couldn't imagine why Cage would protect him, but then Cage's motives were generally a mystery. Smitty showed his true colors when he guessed Cage had bought the lie with a bribe. He'd thought he had grounds for blackmailing the doctor but he'd been afraid to try it until Cage was gone.

I on the other hand guessed that Cage had simply talked the doctor into lying. Freeman had told Cage he had found Smitty shortly before three the night before. Cage had explained that just at that time someone had killed Bea Ella in the Sweet Variety, and pointed out that Smitty would be a prime suspect. Therefore, since it seemed that Smitty must be innocent and yet might well be accused, Freeman agreed to say he had found him even earlier. Probably his agreement was provisional until he heard Harper Gatton corroborate Cage about the time. The doctor had lied in the interests of justice, and not for any bribe.

The question remains of how Cage had known about the murder at eight on Sunday morning, since Gatton hadn't informed him of it until two hours later. What was he doing that night between the time the last witnesses left him on the road and eight the next morning? When I'd heard Cage saying "She was here, screaming at me," I'd assumed he meant Bea Ella and that had only led to confusion. "She" was my mother.

I guessed this much by following a nagging hunch that something about my memory of the murder night was wrong. I felt that a crux of the matter was my entering and leaving my own house. When I thought of entering what I remembered was seeing it strangely lit up so late. I thought about that for a moment, and then it came to me that Horton couldn't have been home asleep as Mother had implied or his light would have been off. Mother had gone out searching for him, not for me, and found him doing something so upsetting that when she'd run into me at home she'd fumbled for a lie rather than reveal the truth even to me. I never knew exactly what she saw. Lucy wasn't there then—maybe Cage and Horton had some of Cage's women, or maybe it was just the two of them.

So Cage and Horton had been at Cage's house while I walked into a trap that had been laid for Cage. He had been meant to find Bea Ella and be accused of murder. And he knew it: he'd known she was in danger and done nothing except stay in public view so he couldn't be accused. He'd known that the deed was done because of the trap he guessed was behind the "letter for Mr. Cage" that had appeared at the hotel before closing. That letter had asked him to come to the Sweet Variety where, it probably claimed, Bea Ella was waiting. Cage rightly guessed that she was already dead and that if he went to the theater in response to the letter he would be charged with her murder. He thwarted the plot by keeping witnesses with him, the whole night, as it happened.

I guessed all this by attending to another of those nagging intuitions. When I thought back on the murder night I kept remembering with uncanny vividness hearing the gurgling of the river as I came out of my house at about 2:45. Something else that nagged me in the same way was my image of Bea Ella calling for help as she realized she was being killed. In my mind's eye I saw her as if she were a figure in a comic strip, her hands raised and though there were balloons coming out of her mouth, nothing was in them but the words "Gurgle, gurgle." I said to myself, "The river's swallowed up her screams," and then with a start I'd seen that if it was still enough for me to hear the river I should have heard Bea Ella.

It meant, simply, that Gatton had lied. There hadn't been any screams for him to hear. He had also lied when he claimed to have discovered me by accident. In fact it was ambush. Gatton had been in hiding on Dock Street, waiting to arrest Cage when he came in response to the letter. But I changed Gatton's plans. Probably I would have been the second choice after Cage for the framing anyway, since Gatton and the other representatives of law and order believed I was to be Cage's heir. And so I was framed. The plot might have succeeded it it hadn't been for the rhinestones.

Rufus had first discovered Bea Ella's body. With the theater locked from the inside to protect himself from the mob in the street, he'd headed toward the rear exit where Bea Ella had presumably left and where he could slip away. Before reaching the door he'd come upon the body, already dead then. When she'd fled into the wings she'd been knocked unconscious or simply collapsed into a drunken sleep. The person who had knocked her out or watched her collapse had left by the rear exit, had returned within the hour to kill her, and had departed the same way, probably only moments before Rufus came in.

When he found Bea Ella Rufus thought better of attracting suspicion by using the rear door. Instead he left by the front, "white as a sheet," locking it carefully. He removed the key behind the fence (he'd known about Lucy's and my meetings) because that night of all nights he didn't want Lucy found in the theater. Then he informed Gatton of his discovery. The two of them had decided to seize the opportunity to do Cage in. They moved Bea Ella into the booth in the lobby so she'd be near Cage when he came in, unlocked the door, and sent the letter. Gatton stationed himself to watch and wait.

Probably Rufus and Gatton both kept themselves from speculating much about who had in fact killed Bea Ella. They may have supposed it was one of the audience in his rage. Perhaps it occurred to one of them to wonder if the other could be guilty. But not even that possibility could deter them in their efforts to reform Wickliffe.

No shred of this information came out at the trial, nor did the fact that I had called Lucy's name when Gatton found me at the theater. Only the official story came out and in fact the trial was something of a joke. I guess by then Gatton and Rufus had given up hope of a conviction. Anyway they were half-hearted in their testimony. I myself told none of what I'd deduced—simply that I hadn't killed her, that I'd noticed the lobby door ajar and so had found her. The jury took thirty minutes before finding me not guilty.

The expressions on the jury's faces made me suspect what was to become more apparent: they and most of the other townspeople actually believed I had done the murder. You might suppose the appearance of some of the rhinestones while I was still in jail would have convinced them otherwise but no, they thought I had been placing them with an accomplice, Horton or someone else. They thought I was offering them all a bribe in the form of a treasure hunt, and they accepted.

They accepted the gems, the excitement of the hunt and the excitement of being privy to successful crime, they accepted vicarious revenge for Bea Ella's souring their pleasure and only they knew what else they accepted. In the months after my acquittal they offered me friendliness and understanding, as they thought. When I wasn't eager for their company they supposed I was troubled by guilt and they redoubled their efforts to console and accept me. At taverns men would offer to buy me drinks and on the street women would smile and flirt cordially, especially if they were wearing the rhinestones.

Rufus profited from the murder. He curtained off the booth, touched it up with chicken blood and charged admission to see it. The Mae West boom was over though. A year or so later he tried showing one of her films and the only audience was a couple of young rivermen who hadn't heard the story and who left when they saw how alone they were. For other movie stars people weren't reluctant to come to the Sweet Variety, but they were quieter.

My public exoneration came five years later. I'd been making a good living hauling cattle and I'd given up troubling myself with thoughts of where Lucy was and what she was doing. I'd lost some wildness, got more substantial, and so had most of Wickliffe including even Horton. But poor Smitty hadn't settled and prospered like the rest of us. After Cage and Lucy left he'd clerked in the hardware store for a while, he'd cut down on the whiskey and bathed and shaved regularly. But the strain was too great. He must have known there wasn't much hope when he lost his clerkship but he did manage to stay honest for another year or two with the odd jobs people gave him out of charity, until he started breaking into houses and stealing, and toward the end he was committing other more sordid and dismal crimes. He seemed to spend most of his time in Harper Gatton's jail. Finally one night he shot himself. He'd done another burglary, he knew Gatton was coming to lock him up again, I guess he decided he'd had enough. He stood on the courthouse steps and fired into the air and when a crowd had gathered he told them that he was the one who had killed Bea Ella Lathrop and scattered her rhinestones. He told them I'd known about it all along, and then he laughed at them and shot himself.

After that, people weren't so friendly to me as before. I could see that some of them resented me, and nobody much wanted my company. I'd assumed I'd be spending the rest of my life there, but now I felt free to leave. I waited three or four months, making up my mind. Mother and Horton were sorry to see me go but they knew it would be harder for everybody if I stayed. I used to visit at Christmas, but since Mother died, and since I've been settled down with a family of my own, I haven't been back at all.

A CHILD OF
THE HEART

THERE ARE STORIES in these mountains of a man whose only
daughter wooed him away from his wife with the cunning that is woman's
part, plucking her heartstrings and dancing before him in the forest. He
was thirty-five years old, old enough to know and guard against the
mind's trickery. We have the story second-, sometimes third-hand, but
we have managed to piece it together in the course of many long evenings
when the talk turns to neighbors and their people. Abram Hodge he was
called, he married a slip of a girl out of Merton County, which is outlaw
country. This place must have been lovely then; there was more rain, and
they say horses died of suffocation, the snows were so deep—though
indeed we have no droughts now: the water falling over that cliff face is
all condensation from the one mountain, Hornet. Hodge's wife was a
Timmons, but she wasn't related to the milk people. He apparently met
her one night in the Blue Moon Café in Arden, a notorious hangout for
prostitutes; and some have said Lula's own morals weren't altogether
Christian before she married Hodge. It was early fall, but she wore a
mouton coat, her pride and joy, in which she was finally buried. Nothing
is known of her forebears. She had flares of that sixteen-year-old insolence
that hides utter desperation.

They swaggered one another right out of the café, up the road and into
the bushes. When he took off his wide leather belt his pants fell straight
off. He was such a sight with his knobby knees and shirttail that Lula
laughed, covering her eyes with one hand and pointing with the other,
whereupon he stepped out of the trousers and brought the belt down

across her bare arm. It couldn't have hurt so much as surprised, but she squealed like a stuck pig. This affected them differently: while it excited him, it sobered her up fast; for one thing, he might have struck her vainglorious face. These two wild youngsters looked at one another in silence for a bit, thinking over that blow and shriek. Without even smiling Hodge then started to draw back his arm for a second swing, and so to protect herself Lula presented: spread her legs and hiked her skirts up to her waist. There was a second pause while Hodge appraised what she had to offer and how she offered it; this must have humiliated her, little knowing he frightened himself, now that he thought about it, as much as he frightened her. Tears flowed down her cheeks and she groaned, kicking her heels into the ground. The belt must have seemed irrelevant. He had her then, and she had him. And at his most vulnerable moment, when all the strength had left his body, she kissed him and said, "I love you, Abram Hodge."

He, expecting her to curse him to the devil once it was over and done with, was moved by love and pity to take her once more in his arms and ask her to be his wife. "I don't care a hoot about money," she said. "It's a good thing," he said, "I've no more to my name than my maternal uncle's house, on Coon Ridge up next to Stacey." "That'll do."

They were married in Pineville, on the road to Stacey. There he bought a mule, a grinning lop-eared animal; it carried Lula up that last mile and a half never traveled by a burdened horse before. Lula wrapped her coat around her and held her head up high, and Hodge beside her smoked a quarter cigar and walked as if the mountain was his.

The house wasn't much—at best it probably had three rooms, a kitchen, a bedroom, and the entrance-hall-parlor that seems so necessary to us. From the truck garden in the back they gathered enough food for Hodge to have to work only four days a week in the mine two valleys over—it's nearly mined out now, but then it was a going concern. He slept in the bunk room there Monday Tuesday and Wednesday nights, and was at home the rest of the time. During the first few long weekends he seldom left his bed, and when he did, it was to turn on the battery-powered radio and dance with Lula, or to chop wood: winter was coming on.

People hereabouts are generally pretty quick family-raisers. It may be because they are powerfully ignorant. It may be because the landscape and the wind make us seem transitory, so that we fling out children the way a spider freely falling emits long coils of web, hoping that some part of it will catch and serve as an anchor. In any case, by the first summer of their marriage they had a daughter. Hodge delivered it himself, which helps to explain his exorbitant affection for the child. Lula refused to have a doctor: "I've seen three babies born and I know as well what to do as any five-dollar liniment man. You just do what I tell you." However, judging by the outcome, something must have gone wrong in the delivery—frightfully wrong, if everything that followed can be traced to that moment.

The first result to be apparent was Lula's subsequent failure to conceive. Although here again she refused a medical examination, the failure was certainly hers. "I can tell you one thing," Hodge said at the time, "I've done my part, and more too," and, as it happens, there was later proof of his fertility. He was displeased at first, wishing, as all men will, to have a son; but since he reckoned that each additional child would add a day to his week's work load, he ended in the belief that the advantages of the situation outweighed the disadvantages.

But Lula was disgruntled. As deeply as she had relished carrying and giving birth to the child, she resented her barrenness. She cried out against it to Hodge as if he might cure it. "At least I'd like to have the choice!" Furthermore, she would only view it as temporary. Hodge's good humor in the face of this seeming misfortune probably suggested to her that somehow he had tricked her in order to enjoy himself without paying the consequences. And he did enjoy himself; he talked about it. Whereas before she had refused him on every third occasion, acting on a personal code of propriety, now she begged for it, two, sometimes three times a day. But years passed, and she seemed to grow resigned.

Meanwhile the daughter Avis grew from infant to child. It was clear from the beginning that she would look nothing like her parents. Both of them were lean and dark by nature, though Lula bleached out her hair and glorified it with a henna rinse; both were meager in the face and Hodge particularly looked as if his cheekbones had been shattered. But Avis the daughter was white-headed and fat—not monstrous, but very plump, and her eyes were small. She appeared, they say, to be made for love.

Again unlike her parents, this Avis wasn't a talker; in fact five years passed before she spoke her first sentence, "I do so love these blackberries." Her second was a better introduction: "Who do you love most, Lula, Abram or me?" Lula gave her food for thought. "Strictly speaking, I don't *love* anybody, but Abram gives me . . ." and here she employed an obscene expression. Avis said very little thereafter, so that we have no way of knowing why she acted as she did; it must all be conjecture with her. She was deep. There is a photograph of her (yes, poor as they were, they had an old Kodak) at six years, according to the inscription; she is squatting somewhere in the woods, wearing dark glasses and nursing a corncob pipe.

This is Hodge's mouth organ; it was auctioned with the other articles left in his house. We find that merely to touch it summons pictures of them, Hodge stripped to the waist, resting after plowing his bony land, drunk with spring water, bending like a woman to adjust his daughter's ruffles; Lula relaxes with the churn between her legs and weaves her hair into a long braid. Far below them is the green valley they disdain; from their house, Old Squaw fifteen miles to the southwest would appear level with them, though it is several hundred feet higher. Surely at this time they were as content as people here have a right to be, especially Hodge, for Lula was after all a pretty thing; like the mule she was a hard worker, and in the eight years of their married life she had shown no inclination to cuckold him. Still, we sometimes wonder whether they, like characters in a soap opera, were living a lie and, if so, whether the success of the ruse depended on Hodge's treating Avis like a son—not that he thought of her as male ("More flounces, more trim," he commanded when Lula was making dresses for the child) but that he took her for that direct spiritual heir a man requires, and so grew confused in his mind. Assuming our suspicions to be justified, it is yet not likely that Hodge was ever aware of the force animating his family. These things can only be understood by strangers, and much later. Hodge and his family doubtless moved in a blur of misguided explanations to their end. Nor does our understanding of him light in any way our own obscurities; but others who are children now in other valleys will make of us the sport and idle puzzle for a winter evening.

Torrential rain and the cloth merchant came together in April of Hodge's family's tenth year. People say the moon causes the inordinate precipitation that plagues us every fifteen and three-quarters years almost to the day. The last was in November, snow, which does less damage than the rain, melting as it does through a period of months. The next will be in August, and will destroy most roads and bridges. Hodge of course had laid in a week's provisions—salt, pork, beans, flour—though the rain usually lasts but three days. He and Lula looked forward to the storm because it would be an obstruction to divert for a moment the smooth flow of their lives, and because it gave Hodge an excuse for laying off work. He was sitting on the porch playing some mountain song on his mouth organ when the yard-goods man arrived. High wind had just started to blow up a drizzle; the typical dense cloudbank grazing Squaw's summit made seeing difficult, so that for some time—perhaps two hours—Hodge watching the figure toil up the footpath was unable to tell anything about it, even its sex. Still he had plenty of time to consider the significance of any intrusion upon his household. Perhaps with visitors so scarce he assumed that the stranger bore ill tidings and so was thrown off his guard when he discovered that it was merely a salesman, and old, probably forty-five years old.

His name was Pike, and he worked out of Johnson City for Sears Roebuck or some such firm. No company would take the trouble to send people up here now, but extravagances like that were common in those days, when they were first getting their hold on us. He was on his first assignment to these parts. He worked this area for four or five years or so, but with him as with Avis we must rely on our imaginations: he never said a word about Hodge and his family. Considering the part he played, his reticence is understandable.

He had held any number of jobs in his lifetime—he may be dead now, of course—and this probably recommended him to Sears Roebuck: at that time convincing the mountain women to order fancy printed cloth instead of using flowered feed sacks demanded considerable resourcefulness. Pike was a strange looker (most of us remember seeing him). He had a barrel torso but thin arms and legs which wobbled as though they weren't properly connected. For a nose he had a wide duck's bill. We attend him so carefully because it has become almost axiomatic that without him the family would have been ordinary and never discussed. He carried a suitcase with the few necessities of his toilet, and a flat book with swatches of cloth for pages. These were mostly cotton goods, bright and boldly patterned. In fact, the man played a large part in forming the taste of our parent's generation and thus of many generations to come. He was a fine talker, and laughed at everything he said. He was laughing as he approached the porch where Hodge sat playing his mouth organ, laughing perhaps at how easy he knew it would be to handle this simple mountaineer, laughing maybe at his own hard-heartedness in taking such undue advantage. But he laughed and shook his head and stumbled over the first step; and, before Hodge had even found out who the man was, he was laughing too.

"Why, I've walked all the way up this contrary mountain to sell you and the wife some printed cottons, summer and winter weight," he said, chuckling as he stepped into the parlor with his arm over Hodge's shoulder. "Pike's the name."

Avis was about ten years old then. The only adults she had ever seen were her parents and the schoolteacher, a woman. She must have weighed near 120 pounds. When Pike entered she lay on the settee at the front window, where she had watched his approach. She was ruffled and beribboned in her customary fashion. If Pike took any notice of her at that moment he must have found the extravagance of her costume a good omen. When Avis smiled, she pressed her tongue against the back of her teeth. The schoolteacher said she was but a mediocre student. In her idle hours she had whittled numerous small heads of soft pine, and strung them together to wear as a necklace.

Lula too had watched the stranger's advance for a long time, but as he drew near she retreated to the kitchen (thinking it indecorous for the whole family to be caught gaping); so that Hodge was obliged to summon her from pretended baking and watch her smooth her apron with hands just dipped into the flour bin. She curtsied, out of instinct evidently; she had never done it before.

By the time she had offered him a spot of tea and prepared it, the rain was heavy and thick, like a waterfall blown over the house. Luckily Hodge had a sheet tin roof with doubled tarpaper beneath it. As they watched the boiling tea flow from the pitcher spout into a cup, Hodge and Lula together realized the importance of the storm, which had arrived seven hours too early. Far from merely being rude, sending Pike away during the next three days would mean taking the responsibility for his probable death. Now Hodge knew that this must have dawned on Lula when it dawned on him, and he said he glanced up at her, and something must have been on her mind already, because she didn't look at him at all but passed the cup to Pike calmly as if the sun were shining outside. Hodge said he scratched his head and screwed up his mouth and thought, but there was nothing for it, Pike would have to stay. Meanwhile the first rush of water was bringing down loose rubble that had accumulated on the slopes in the previous fifteen and three-quarters years. Through the rain they could hear it crash and grind. Hodge explained the situation to Pike, telling him it wouldn't be safe to leave the homestead. Pike said it was typical of his luck to happen on this misfortune, but he doubted whether he would still be selling cloth when the next storm came.

One of the difficulties associated with our small houses is the lack of any privacy. This means, for instance, that every child hears, often sees, his parents in the act of love, though we all try to wait until the children are asleep. Perhaps this seems improper, but so far as we can tell it is seldom harmful. However it may well have affected Avis's mind, since Lula was doubtless a screamer. The rain during Pike's visit made even a short talk outside between Hodge and Lula impractical, and they were both too polite by nature to whisper in the house, even during the night, though they no more curtailed their lovemaking than fasted. It was the first time in their married life that they had been so deprived of conversation, and they felt the privation, especially Hodge. In fact, without Pike they probably would have used these days of rain to speak thoughts otherwise relinquished to silence. As it was, they confronted him without coming to an agreement about him.

Night drew on, and Hodge cleared his throat to tell Lula to make up a pallet bed in the parlor for Pike, who said it would be fine—he had slept on everything from railroad cars to junk piles, and he said he didn't think he was meant for comfort.

Throughout, Avis watched without a word, and as was her habit

39

raised the necklace to hold a few of the smiling faces in her mouth. Hodge fluffed up her pinafore and beamed with pride at the stranger. Lula boiled pork and turnip greens for dinner. As they sat at the small kitchen table Pike made them laugh with his demonstrations of the way Alabama migrant workers eat. Hodge and his family began to think that a few days with Pike might be very pleasant, even though he never ceased his sales talk, suggesting dotted Swiss for Avis's dresses, robin's-egg gingham for Lula, flowered wool for Hodge's ties, red and white oilcloth for the table; but he was never disagreeable. Lula decided to order several dollars' worth from him. Pike saw that Hodge and Lula did not address Avis, and he followed suit; but there must have been a peculiar roll to his eyes when he regarded her. Men like him have ways.

There is dispute yet about what exactly happened and how, not to mention why. Pike's visit was the only section of Hodge's life he showed any reluctance to discuss with his fellow miners. Consequently we have to supplement the facts we have received. It has been a thankful task. Our version has a strong claim to truth, a strong claim, for we have lived here; our blood flowed in Hodge's veins; we have common ancestors. More important, the tale has persisted almost unchanged for a decade now. It has become for us undeniable as a song that is born slowly among our people.

The events of the first night were subtle and quiet; in fact, it is only in retrospect that they appear as events at all. Pike settled down on his pallet, smiling and chuckling a bit. The rain had abated, as it always does after about eight hours. Avis did not sleep immediately, but lay still and rolled her eyes in the dark. When Hodge came to touch Lula he noticed she was slow—not reserved exactly but careful, slow and thoughtful. Her mind had probably turned again to the birth of her daughter and the subsequent barrenness. As we have said, they did not speak.

The second day's confinement made everyone fidgety. They had absorbed the novelty of the situation, which now seemed to require a festivity as commemoration, and so Hodge played a wild jig, and Lula danced with Pike, flushed and laughing. Her loins would have shown their contours through her meager cotton dress. It was not cold, and a fire kept the damp off. Avis sat on the floor in the corner and snapped her fingers, bounding her corkscrew curls. The dimples in her cheeks were deep and large as navels. Then after a time Pike played the mouth organ —indifferently, Hodge said—and Lula danced with Hodge. This was in the morning; the afternoon was quieter, though Avis continued to snap her fingers and perform little dances with her hands. The lull would have lasted through supper had Pike not roused himself to draw on his fund of tall tales. Lula watched the floor. Hodge said it occurred to him that Pike might have had a courting urge toward her, but that he never suspected her of thoughts of infidelity. Be that as it may, Hodge did not at the time watch the stranger very carefully, nor did he afterwards give the incident much importance. It is we who connect Pike with the catastrophe of five years later.

Hodge was tired, and went to sleep soon. Pike, Lula and Avis lay wide awake and very quiet. Doubtless they all trembled slightly. After two hours Lula rose from her bed and wrapped a mackintosh around her to go outside to the outhouse. It was in the back yard, but to reach it she had to go through the parlor and out the front. Pike heard the bedroom door open, and the hesitant tread of bare feet. The darkness was so intense that he could not distinguish the silhouette of the figure. He breathed as if he were asleep, and kept watch so that as Lula opened the outer door he recognized her against the dim cloudbank. When she ran out through the rain, he smiled to himself and passed his hand over his face. She had done nothing definite yet to betray herself, but he was the sort of man who can predict what a woman will do, and he laughed quietly.

Lula waited in the outhouse for a time, hearing only the rain, feeling it drip slowly, much like tears, through the leak in the roof. It was during these minutes that she considered, if at all, the morality of what she was about to do. As we have said, she had reason to believe she was right, but she was not one to mind much if she was wrong. When she returned to the house she came softly to Pike's pallet, and stood listening to him, trying to see him. She knew from Hodge's snore that he was asleep. She didn't give a thought to Avis.

After a while she realized that Pike was feigning sleep. There was a little catch of laughter in his regular breath. She nudged him with her toe, but he just whinnied and shifted his weight. Then she knelt and laid her hands between his legs. At first he didn't move, but finally he said, "Tomorrow night," and then he rolled over and hid his face in the pillow. There was nothing for Lula to do except go back to her own bed. Supposedly Avis could see in the dark, like a cat; she must have watched her mother's face very carefully. This was the second night.

The third day was the stillest, with Lula hardly daring to move. She sewed, and kept pricking her lips with the needle. Hodge had begun to frown, and he noticed a few glances between Pike and Lula, a touch of their hands at dinner—suspicious things never quite concrete enough to justify turning the stranger out. Of course it was Pike's intention that Hodge should be suspicious. But that conniver was working much more destruction than he knew, for it was at these moments that Hodge's wrong-headed reliance on Avis came up in him most charac-

41

teristically: he tried to distract her attention, because he was ashamed for *her*, as though she were a son, or a man friend, seeing him cuckolded. He felt that before her he had to save face, when she, a girl, and nothing like him, nor caring a whit for dignity maintained, would have been only too happy to see Lula and the stranger slip arm in arm off into the night, never to return. She saw the opportunity of besting her mother, and she must have trembled, soft and wet clear through; so that she would not take her eyes from Lula. Thus Hodge thought, "She doesn't even have the courtesy to pretend not to notice," and since he thought she must be scorning him in her mind, and vaunting herself above him, he turned on her and struck her for not listening when he spoke. This was the only blow she ever received from him.

That night when they blew out the lanterns Hodge stayed as alert as everybody else, he too pretending to sleep. Lula may have realized that he was awake beside her, but she was past the point of minding. Near midnight again she rose and threw on the slicker to go out. The rain had begun to clear. As she passed Pike she gave him a solid kick and then in the doorway beckoned for him to follow. She waited in the outhouse. Meantime Hodge had decided it behooved him to investigate, and came tiptoeing into the parlor. If he heard a slight rustling he assumed it was one of the rats or squirrels that often took refuge beneath the floor. He reached Pike's pallet, hesitated, and plunged his hand down, and found the bed empty. He didn't bother to fetch the shotgun, but merely ran.

In the gloomy outhouse Lula heard the splashing steps and began to caress her lips. When the door flew open she gasped and embraced the figure, recognizing her husband as she kissed him. "Where is he?" Hodge said. He shook her. "I'll pull his goggle eyes from his face!"

"He's not here, Abram," she said. "He's in his bed."

"Woman, you lie," he said, and struck her, and went to search outside. He was in time to catch a glimpse of the peddler with his satchel loping through the darkness down the path away from the house; he had clearly just come out the front door. Hodge hailed him, but Pike seemed not to hear. Within a minute he was out of sight, and the sound of his feet obscured by the rain. Lula, cowering in the shed, decided that since she would eventually have to show herself, it might as well be at once. Hodge stood in the yard, soaked to the skin, his hands in his pockets, his head cocked to the side in bewilderment. There had simply not been time for the stranger to make it out to Lula and back to the house, even assuming he had packed his belongings in advance, which he had in fact done. Lula summoned her courage and approached him, saying, "You've wronged me, Abram Hodge, grievously. In your heart of hearts you know it. In all our years of marriage I have never looked at another man."

"Why did he leave?" Hodge said.

Ultimately, Hodge and Lula attributed Pike's hasty departure to the oddity of his mind. When they returned to the house they asked Avis whether she had been awake to hear him go. "Yes," she said, "he only told me goodbye, and then he went." They were puzzled as well that in the following years, although Pike came to the region, he never visited their house again. Hodge thought they might have said something to offend him, but could not imagine what it was. With Hodge it was probably regard for his daughter, and with Lula pride, that kept the truth from them. Pike did not actually violate Avis, for though she was but ten she would surely have conceived and borne wonderful offspring, a true child of the heart to grace the mountain; the fruit of Pike's action was less tangible. We suppose that while Hodge and Lula were outside, as he had planned, Pike did something in the nature of showing himself, or viewing Avis, but we're not eager to know the unpleasant details. It is likely that each one who hears the story has his private version of the occurrence, imagining the laughing peddler and the silent girl together, in the dark; but we are reticent here. Men like Pike are often very inventive. Nor does it surprise us that he was drawn to the child more than to the woman; we too can appreciate the power of copious flesh.

There has been some conjecture in the foregoing, but the rest is a matter of history. Ask anyone here and they will say the same. Hodge and Lula should have hypothesized more about Pike's visit, because the words, "He only told me good-bye, and then he went," were the last to pass Avis's lips. Lula beat her after months of silence, and she responded with but a dull blush. Her parents continued to send her down to the school, hoping she would be forced into speech there, but the teacher complained that she would not even communicate in writing.

That feeble old crow perched in the shadows there above the mantlepiece belonged to Avis. In the spring after Pike's visit Lula took it as a baby from its nest and fed it sugar and milk from an eyedropper. A crow will speak if its tongue is split when it is young. Lula asked Hodge to do it. She said, "You're good with a knife, Abram." She held the beak open while he divided the little strip of flesh before Avis's greedy eyes. It seems particularly intelligent. Hodge and Lula found it would learn almost anything, and so as much for their own amusement as for Avis's they taught it a multitude of sentences, the better part of which don't bear repeating. It was talkative then, but now it does little more all day long than shift its weight from foot to foot, as now. Doesn't it look wise, through, with the fire on those purple feathers and in its eyes. Its beak was yellow once. We feed it leftovers from the table. They're long-lived. It was Avis's pet, and Hodge and Lula left the naming of it up to her, as an added incentive to speech, so that to this day it is simply known as the crow. It has learned from everyone.

Hodge was deeply affronted by his daughter's silence, and he talked to her many long hours, begging her to make an effort, to be reasonable. We imagine that he had his moments of fury, chopping wood or walking alone on the mountain, when he thought of the plight to which stubbornness had reduced his only child. He had not dressed her since birth in bright colors and flounces to see her languish ignored. He had dreamt that the most eligible county rakes would come courting and scraping to his front door; he had hoped to laugh at them with Avis; he had expected grandsons the more strapping for his lack of sons. But he would not have shown his anger to the girl; his heart melted before her. Lula bore the brunt, and transmitted it increased.

During the four days of the week when Hodge was away at work she used the child like an animal, knowing her crimes would not be reported. As Lula lay in her bed in the darkness thinking, a rage would come upon her and she would rise and take a belt from the wall or a flyswatter to beat Avis, reaching forward between blows to determine the position of the body. Avis would have run away had she known any place to go. Occasionally Lula had accesses of kindness or perhaps pity, which she demonstrated as her rage; but they were rare.

Inevitably some of the less desirable country boys came to court the girl. They soon learned not to call when Hodge was home, for he turned them out, every one, after a scornful appraisal: not good enough for his daughter. He said there were some humiliations to which he would not stoop. Lula on the other hand, scorning them even more than Hodge, forced them on Avis, encouraged them with improper suggestions. Avis would fight these suitors while Lula turned her back, or retired to the outhouse, ignoring the noises of battle. But Avis was strong, and weighed near 250 pounds, and thus was able to preserve her chastity, sustaining no injuries worse than torn clothing, which Lula quickly repaired against Hodge's return.

The crow was Avis's only companion during these years. It appeared to love her as though it could understand her mistreatment. It rested on her shoulder or head as she strolled in the thin pine forest that sloped down the mountain to the left of the house. She must have loved it dearly, and may have spoken to it in secret. Sometimes it crept beneath her skirt and clung to her undergarments, and then Lula would say, "Where's that crow? You've killed it, haven't you, you morbid girl. Killed it to spite me. There'll be no mourning here, Avis, when you seek your grave." Avis would raise one of the wooden heads of her necklace to her mouth, and close her eyes. And if, as often happened, Lula struck Avis, the crow would come tumbling from beneath the girl's skirt and go running away. It has always avoided flying except when it was absolutely necessary.

After a year or two Hodge and Lula gave up hope that even the crow would induce Avis to talk, and the family settled into an equilibrium. When Avis was about fourteen the last of the county boys ceased to call on her, and people said she was destined to die without any man's having tasted the pleasures of her flesh; it would surely have been tragic so. Hodge continued to go to the mines, and Lula to punish Avis, though not so strenuously as before. Avis's silence and apathy slowly communicated itself to her parents. Days would pass without a word uttered in the house, and months without Hodge's mounting Lula; she seemed to have lost her wish for more children, and with it her desire for love. It angered Hodge, but not as it would have done earlier. He took heavily to drink and visited the women of the town in Pineville regularly. In every season Lula spent much of her time beside the window, her hands in her lap. Hodge would stand beside her and hold her head against his stomach, and she would embrace his legs, as if they were the only people on earth..

This quietude is a second state in which Hodge and his family might have ended, not only ignorant of the trouble that was with them, but also without its ever reaching consummation, and so we would have no more than the vaguest rumors of them, a man and his wife and speechless daughter, who once lived up on Coon Ridge. But in the summer of the sixteenth year of her marriage Lula had a second blossoming of beauty and vitality.

There is no explaining why it happened. We remind ourselves that she was evidently of vigorous stock, and the less likely for that to pine and fade away. Also there was the fact that Avis was celebrating her sixteenth birthday, traditionally the most romantic in a girl's life, without a husband or suitor. But above all it must have been that lovely summer that entered Lula's blood; we all remember and gloat over it, telling our children they may never see such weather. Many of us were first in love then, among the sweet william and bleeding hearts, and the mountain laurel everywhere, everywhere, and honeysuckle so thick and sweet you nearly fainted. The memory of those flowers brings tears to our eyes. Only a fool will deny that an abundance of flowers can quicken a woman's blood, and that continuing sun can burn years off a man's back. The poverty of life here augments the power of those influences. We lose our vision, and move like wooden toys: one year we wash the curtains, the next we plant a row of cabbage behind the house; and then comes a summer like that one, with grass soft as rabbit fur, and flowers.

From early June Lula started making shopping trips every Saturday down to Stacey; it was time to spend that mite she had saved through the years. She bought only for herself—ribbons and strips of lace, and one polka-dot sundress. When she first rode into town in her high-heeled shoes the men raised their heads, and the women raised their eyebrows. Not that she was flaunting; she didn't need to. She had come down off the mountain firmer, younger, more alive than any woman Stacey had ever known. She tucked a sprig of lilac behind her ear, and smiled at whoever she met. Sometimes Hodge came with her, and he was her equal, so that the whole town envied them their nights; but more often she came alone, as when she met Pike, who was making his annual assault on Stacey. He stood in front of Durfee's store chewing the fat with some of the men when she stepped onto the porch.

He took one look at her and burst out laughing. "Well, Mrs. Hodge!" he said. "Well, you know, you wouldn't hardly believe it, but as I was telling these gentlemen, I was just getting ready to start up old Coon to pay you folks a visit. Now what do you think of that?"

"Well, Pike," she said, and she was smiling, and laughing too, "why don't you go right ahead. Abram's up at the house, and I expect he'd be tickled to see you." She walked past him cool as a cucumber. He just laughed harder, and took the men with him to the drugstore and bought them all ice-cream sodas. He was seen in Stacey for a few more years after that, and then he disappeared. Treating him that way must have been one of the great pleasures of Lula's life. Durfee says that was the time she bought the sundress.

Hodge's mine began to curtail operations that summer, so that he was at home more than ever. Thrown together, and both of them feeling particularly sprightly, he and Lula quickly began to get wild. He had already, as we have said, taken to drink as consolation, and now he drank more and it made his blood the hotter. It was a three-month spree, and he wasn't one to do things by halves. He ceased altogether to visit the town women. Up on their mountain he and Lula did things unheard-of in these parts; and what's more he described them to the men at the mine. They said he looked like an angel of a boy with his eyes shining at the thought of it, and them encouraging him, grinning at one another and saying "Yes, Abram, tell us about it. Look out, now, Abram," and some of the younger ones walking away in embarrassment. When he left the mine on his way home, he had already forgotten them as they slapped him on the back and said, "Now go to it, Abram." If he reflected at all during these months it must have been to wonder in amazement what cloud had lain on the preceding years.

For the first time he faltered in his attentions to Avis. As never before, the trinkets he brought home were for his wife instead of his daughter. Avis appeared to accept this change as stoically as she had accepted

46

everything else in her life; at the height of Hodge's madness he was able to find no reproach in her face—only her vegetable endurance, which did not anger him as might be expected. He saw with extreme clarity. When he thought of her, noticed her sitting on the floor in the corner, with her legs extended in front of her, he shook his head pensively, seeming to understand her to the bone, or he patted her on the neck, and once he said, "Ah, Avis, life has left you in the lurch." His eyes would have been very clear and wide, without a trace of sorrow; and she would perhaps have looked at him, and then at the crow, and blinked, but reacted in no other way. Lula had lost all interest in the girl, and no longer punished her; when Hodge was away Lula mostly lay outside in the long grass to let the sun warm her, and the breeze stir her hair and clothing.

The summer progressed, and all of them, even Avis whom common sense would have profited, thought it would never end. They had a birthday party for her in July. It began as an island of calm in the midst of the turbulence. Hodge baked the cake himself, a large one. Lula did a job of fancy decorating with icing colored by blueberries and melon juice. Avis realized it was her birthday when they exiled her to the yard so that they could bake in privacy; the crow walked beside her, and when she sat down to think it gamboled about her, stalking butterflies between the long blades of grass, turning its head to speak to her. She still had springing gold corkscrew curls.

It should have been a fine celebration of the season and of Avis's womanhood; it could have been peace for the family, and harmonious rest. But Hodge and Lula would not desist. He poured himself a cup of elderberry wine, and she held the tube of frosting with which she adorned the cake, and caressed it, and squirted it lasciviously into her mouth. He took her by the hair into the bedroom, and so they played and drank until mid-afternoon, while Avis waited outside. No doubt it was hunger that finally drove them to finish the cake and summon her. At four o'clock there were still four hours of light left. The honeysuckle is stronger in the evening because of the heat and water in the air; this sweetest and heaviest of summer odors comes from the throats of the most delicate blossoms, scattered like short-lived insects along the vine. One year none of our animals reproduced because a blight had destroyed the honeysuckle.

We suppose that Hodge made a final commitment to his illusion that afternoon; impelled by alcohol and the weather, and his splendid manhood, he closed his eyes authoritatively to the fact that Avis was his, and that she was female and therefore demanded at least the pretense of attention, without which (again because she was assuredly a woman, that fat girl) she would grow devious and perhaps vindictive—that like all women good and bad she had an instinct to discover a man's vulnerable

47

place and strike him there. It is never pleasant when a man and his daughter go wrong. Our sympathies are with him and Lula even though we know perfectly well that Avis suffered more. We don't pretend to understand the girl, but were we in Hodge's place, or Lula's, we would have been kinder and more wary. Still, we realize that they were mightily passionate and blinded. Here it is easy to become lost for a lifetime in isolated errors or special predicaments. He had a good time of it, though, Hodge, while it lasted. He left no progeny, so that his story will soon die away. Even now it is almost exclusively our property, and only we cherish these relics, the mouth organ and the crow. Nothing of Lula's is left, and nothing of Pike's, should we want it.

They lit the candles in broad daylight, and called Avis in, laughing and beaming, expecting her to be overjoyed to find the cake and a ribbon or two for her hair, Hodge ready to cut, and Lula standing behind him disheveled and shining with sweat, unable to still her hands. Hodge played Happy Birthday, Avis blew out the candles, and they each ate a slice of cake. Then Lula just wandered out onto the porch, and Hodge took a jug of hard cider and followed her, leaving Avis alone. She sat at the table and fed the crow tidbits of icing, and doubtless the seeds of her idea came to her then.

She little could predict how favorable the circumstances would be. On the porch Hodge began by playing some of the slower melancholy songs. Lula sang with him, resting her head on his shoulder. The sun slipped down the cleft between Squaw and the more distant Brame; the air cooled and stirred a bit; there is usually some whip-poor-will, even so high, that calls before dusk. Hodge finished the cider, and fetched a fifth of bourbon from the kitchen, twice passing Avis without a sign of recognition. Only her eyes moved, watching him lurch and stumble against the furniture. "Damn fool," the crow screamed, as he returned to the porch, and Hodge laughed a loud free laugh that seemed to travel in a spiral up to the evening's first stars. He fell to the steps, and began to play "Turkey in the Straw" or "She'll Be Coming Round the Mountain," a lively air, interrupting himself to drink or shout. Wisteria hung from the porch roof. Lula snapped her fingers, tossed her head, then held her hair away from the back of her neck; she leaned against one of the uprights. Her sighs became her, and the moonlight. Hodge's brain was spinning when he felt her hand on his thigh, and looked up at her drawn lovely face descending; he reached out for her, but she smiled and was away, rolling across the lawn with her arms entwined above her head. He ran and sank to cover her, and found only the sweet grass. She knelt beside him, moving her hand in his hair as though it were water, and then fled, before he could catch her, laughing, into the wood.

That stand of pine on Coon is no more than a mile square, and sparsely

48

settled; but it served for mischief. Mountain pines are almost as large as those in the valleys, because of the snow that lingers later here, often into May. They are fragrant and shadowy, in moonlight a blue, black green. Rain washes away the mat of needles every year, so that thick grass grows beneath the trees. Hodge followed Lula, tripping, falling into the pine boughs, calling her, shouting what he would do when he caught her. At first she kept within his sight, and then she completely lost herself, for she was delirious.

A spray of needles crossed Hodge's face (they are tender until late August) and he stopped and held them in one hand, kissing them and saying words of love as he undressed. Of course the air was still warm. A fine sight he must have been, dancing and singing stark naked between the trees, his bottle of bourbon wreathing him in its own scent. He circled and backtracked, halloed and cursed, and soon had lost his clothes as well as Lula. Now and again he heard footsteps, and then the fire in him grew unbearable, and he charged after the sound, tearing himself against branches and bark. He would have taken anything, human or animal, but most of all he wanted Lula, because the season and the woods put him in mind of their first meeting. The same idea may have been in her head, as she followed him, guided by his cries, intending to stay away from him until it was no longer possible, and then reveal herself, surrender; it must have seemed to her that she had the power of miracles. When Hodge's calls stopped she thought he had heard her coming behind him, and was now stalking her, so that she turned and crept away from him, smiling, trembling.

But Hodge had forgotten her. Who knows what he thought he saw in the clearing before him, if he thought at all, for the briefest moment—a mountain nymph, a gift from the Lord to requite his trials, some rare and thankful creation of the alcohol? But she was real, and she was his daughter, and mad as he was he should have known it, but he didn't. She stood tiptoe with her back to him, in full moonlight, swaying. She too was naked, naked all that flesh the sun had never touched, white as snow. She had graced herself with flowers, sweet peas and columbine woven in a coronet, chains of red clover slung from her neck and waist—she wore only flowers.

Knowing he wanted her, she rolled her hips, slapping them with her open palms. Hodge stepped forward, and then halted as she turned slowly, exposing the wealth of her body. She had painted her face so that is was hardly recognizable, should he notice it. It apparently surprised her to find him naked, and so ready for love, for her swaying stopped and she covered herself with the demure gesture of a pagan statue. This was irresistible incitement, and Hodge forced her to her back and violated her. We see this outrage from above, through the eyes of the crow, who watched in the shadows of one of the surrounding pines. Naturally we do not dwell long or often on that hateful embrace lapped in the long grass, Avis all white and Hodge white below the waist, the eyes of each searching those of the other. Avis seems to have had fits and spasms of conscience: one minute she participated wholeheartedly, and the next she tried feebly to slide from beneath him, but he followed close on her. Lula either found them there, or surmised the truth when she returned to the empty house. She fell on her bed and slept.

Hodge was a long time having done with Avis—he left her, drank some bourbon to refresh himself, and returned for more. When he was finally finished for good he departed bowing and blowing kisses, to find his clothes. A little later Avis entered the house looking normal, calm as you please, and took her own bed without a glance at her mother. Hodge could not find his clothes; in the course of his search he came again to the place where he had seen the vision of loveliness and, seized with desire, he spent most of the night searching for her, until near dawn he fell from exhaustion and slept till noon.

This was the night, then, that was Abram Hodge's undoing. When he awoke he could remember the body but not the face of the creature he had met in the moonlight. He assumed it was an alcoholic mirage, and told his friends at the mine, from whom we have the facts. Some of them suspected the truth behind his blithe revelations; and they, as we, yearned to see the daughter, merely to see the perpetrator of such a monstrosity, and perhaps then be able to guess what words she spoke in her mind during the act, and whom she abhorred afterwards. But Avis revealed no clue to her secret.

Then for two months—she allowed two—Lula was the motive force in the family. She was cunning and careful, and things happened as she planned. Her guilt is great, that is clear; but by the time she assumed control there was little she could do honorably other than carry to conclusion the pattern she had discovered. She was by no means a bad woman—Lula was able to see her situation in but a single light. God rest her soul. During those two months she loved Hodge more passionately and tenderly than ever before; he had come to seem like a child to her. She lived only for him, and to watch Avis like a hawk. Of course two months was far more than she needed: perhaps she was offering the Lord a chance to intervene, or perhaps she thought Avis might take matters into her own hands.

It was an overcast morning in August, with the cold clouds low enough to surround Hodge's cabin like mist. He was away at the mines. Lula rose from her bed in her flannel nightdress and took a hammer and beat Avis in the stomach to destroy the new life there; Avis doubtless made no attempt to protect herself and her child, but merely watched her mother's stern face. Then Lula hanged herself in the parlor, and Avis rose and ran outside—she too in her nightclothes. She whirled and pirouetted through the pine woods and over Coon's west cliff face, now known as Avis's Jump. When Hodge returned two days later and found Lula, he hurried down the mountain and away, evidently without a thought of his daughter. Nothing has been heard of him since; he could still be alive somewhere. Lula was given a Christian burial but, because Avis had done an unholy thing, no one has ever disturbed her remains, in the gorge of rock where they lie. With the passage of years her skull has somehow grown enormous. Moss covers her teeth; swallows nest and wheel in the eyes; a young pine has sprouted through the cavern that was her nose, and in time will shatter the bone. A neighbor took charge of selling the house and goods—it was then that we bought the mouth organ, and the crow, who had not followed Avis out in her last wild dash, but had wisely remained in the house, brooding, and guarding Lula until Hodge came.

THE VACATION

IF I CUT across Moose Zacham's barnyard on my way to town, he won't speak. If I go over to the courthouse to pass some time, even old Lucian that sweeps ignores me. Of an evening I tip my hat to the people on their porches, or those I meet on the road, but they act like they don't see me. I'm nearly fifty years old, I've always lived here—I know it was partly wrong what I did, but I don't deserve this. It makes me not know what to do with myself. It makes me not see how I'm going to manage the rest of my days. It's worse now than it was in the fall, because there's nothing to do but look after the cow and chickens. After dark I stoke me up a good fire and listen to Paducah on the radio a while before I go to bed. I've figured out one thing: people would have forgiven me it all if only I hadn't come to their doors the way I did.

My Blanche and our boy Howard stay at the hotel—Blanche's brother Bailey Carlisle runs it, and he gives them room and board. I haven't run into them for two or three weeks. The last time, they crossed to the other side of the street when they saw me coming. Frisky?—she looked friskier than ever, stepping right along with her nose in the air. She had on the black floppy hat she used to wear when we were courting. Howard was so embarrassed I thought he was going to fall on his face. I stood and watched them till they turned the corner and in spite of everything I couldn't help laughing. The house does seem empty without them, but it's not being able to talk to people that bothers me more. Blanche and Howard always seemed sort of like children to me.

Last February was Howard's twenty-first birthday and Blanche's fortieth. That gave me an excuse to do something I'd been studying about for a good while—have a kind of vacation for a whole year. I had forty-three hundred-dollar bills in a coffee can down next to the southeast cornerstone doing me no good, and besides we had more than a year's provisions for ourselves and the animals, so I guessed we could afford a slack year. Most people go see relatives or take a trip through the Blue Ridge Mountains on their vacations, but I wasn't interested in any such thing. I'd had a lot of ideas floating around in my head for a long time, and I wanted to stay right here and get them straight and worked out. And anyway there were odds and ends I wanted to see about at my leisure. On Howard's birthday I told them I'd have a surprise for them, and on Blanche's I told them what it was.

She started in talking about where we could go but I said no, I was staying put but they could go anywhere they wanted, and for them to think it over, take their time, because they had a year anyway, so there was no cause to fly off the handle yet. I said we'd each have seven hundred dollars to spend however we wanted during the year, no strings attached, and they'd have my love and my blessing to do what they wanted, so long as they didn't interfere with me doing what I wanted, and I wanted to start off by thinking and not running off somewhere.

Howard thought it was a joke at first—he just laughed and shook his head, and he said, "That's a good one." But Blanche knew better: she looked hard at me and then she said, "Listen here, Louis, what is it you mean to think about, I'd like to know?" I said I myself wasn't sure yet, but I'd let her know as I got it worked out. Then I gave them the money. Howard began to realize I was serious about it, and he said, "I'll have to hand it to you, Daddy, you've really done it this time!" Blanche started to perk up too—"Well," she said, "I guess I could use a new dress or two, at that." "Sure you could," Howard said. "Why you know you could, Mother. Boy oh boy, this is really something!" Blanche said, "I can't help it, though, the whole thing does make me a little nervous. Just give me a few days to get over it—it's such a surprise, and I've never heard of anything like it." "I never have either," I said. "It's real nice of you," she said, and Howard said, "Lord, 'nice' ain't even the word for it!" I felt good, awful good that night when we blew out the lamps.

The vacation started the next day at breakfast. Blanche said, "Now Louis, let's talk this over a little more. I can't really figure out what we're meant to do. I'd like to get a better idea of what you have in your mind."

"Well," I said, "I'm not exactly sure myself—I thought we could all figure it out ourselves, you know. What you're *meant* to do is whatever you *want* to do."

"Well now listen," she said. "Supposing I wanted to go off somewhere and you didn't: I don't see how I could, because who'd get your food for you and Howard, and so forth?"

Howard said, "Lord, I hadn't thought of that."

"Let's think about it, then," I said. I was curious to see what they would do. I felt like smiling at their timidity. I was timid too, or nervous at least, but it wasn't about who was to get my food for me!

I think Howard was afraid I might change my mind if any difficulties came up, because he said, "Wait a minute, now. If you took a trip somewhere, Mother, why we could fix our own meals, after all. We could buy our own butter and cheese, you know, there's no reason we couldn't. And if I went somewhere too, Daddy could do the same. Land, we could even hire Judy Dowdy for instance to come and take care of him, and I could hire Pete Corum to give him what help he needed with the work, and he wouldn't be needing much. He did say we could do what we wanted with the money." He looked at me out of the corner of his eye to see whether I approved or nor, and Blanche was looking like she hoped I wouldn't.

I said, "I see I need to say a little more about this. This idea of mine: I want it to be the best thing in the world for all of us. But the point of it is, it has to depend on us, on each one, how it turns out. And even though when you first thought about it you might not have noticed it—you, Howard, especially—I expect problems. I mean it may not be as easy as it seems. For my part, anyway, I don't expect to know what it was until it's all over. We're having a vacation so we can *do* something, and if it's worth doing it's bound to be some trouble. Myself, I'll doubtless be up to things you couldn't imagine right now.

"Anyway," I said, "let's not for heaven's sake bog ourselves down with worrying about how we're to get food in our mouths. Each can see to his own. And you're not to pay for mine out of the money I gave you to pay for yours! And, Blanche, sweetheart, unless you have a particular yen to be at the stove, why you needn't even think about meals. Now you all do what you want today—you might start making some serious plans—I've put out paper and pencils in the parlor in case you want to write anything down."

Blanche said, "Well, I guess so . . . but what are you going to do now?"

"Well, I said, "what I'm going to do right now is, I'm going to walk over into the woods."

"Why, the hunting season hasn't even started!"

"I know," I said, "I'm just going. I don't even know what I'm going to do when I get there."

Blanche said, "I never heard of such a thing!"

"I know," I said.

They looked almost scared, so I held both their hands for a minute, and then I left them staring at me as I walked out.

I went to a place I'd stumbled onto once before. It was the kind of place I'd have liked when I was a boy—and I just wanted to spend some time there. The time I found it, the dog chased a rabbit back through some underbrush and then couldn't get back out, so I had to fight my way through to get to him. The opening had grown over, so I knew nobody had been there. When you get through the thicket you come to a sort of little clearing with big old shady maples and wild crabapple and black-berry and a little creek. It made me feel peaceful. I stretched myself out on a shelf of rock, and I thought awhile. The birds were singing and the stream was rippling, and the sandstone was warm from the sun. Fifty yards or so downstream there was a little hidden lake—I could hear a fish jump now and then. I decided that before the year was out I'd have to have a swim there. I talked to myself for a while. I said, "Now what shall I do with this year, after all?" because I myself didn't know yet. "Well," I said, "no need to rush, is there? No, no need to rush." Then I said, "You know, maybe I'll *make* something." I thought I might want to build me a cabin all my own out there in the woods, like Henry David Thoreau did at Walden Pond. I thought about that, and then I had a nap.

I spent the rest of the day walking around in the woods. When I got home, only Blanche was there—she'd been in to town and bought herself some dresses and a pair of shoes. Howard had gone over to Dawson with his buddies. Blanche was kind of quiet, but she perked up when I got her to try on her new clothes for me. We turned on the radio and did a waltz in the parlor. She said, "Have you decided what you want to do?" I said, "No, have you?" and she said no she hadn't yet, but she thought she might visit her folks in Louisville. I told her I thought the best thing would be for her to go on ahead, if she really wanted to, and then maybe I'd come later.

For about a week she dilly-dallied, making up her mind, and then she decided to go. I helped her as best I could. I knew I'd miss old Blanche—we hadn't been apart for more than a day or two since we'd been married—but I have to say I was glad to see her finally go, because I felt like I needed to do some thinking on my own. Howard meantime was spending most of his time carousing over in Dawson like I expected he would. The day after Blanche left he showed up with a used car he'd bought, and said he and Jimmie Thorne were going to drive down to Nashville. I told him to watch out for gambling and women, and I gave him my blessing.

II

The day after Howard left I went into town for the first time since

Blanche's birthday. I thought I'd best take care of having my food sent to me and so forth right away, so I wouldn't have to bother about it. I met Otho Keezer in the grocery, and he said, "Well, now, Louis, it's good to see you up and about again," and he clapped me on the back. I had no idea what he meant—I thought he was joking, so I just laughed and went on about my business. But when others kept asking me if I was better, I started asking them what they meant, and that way I finally got to the bottom of it: before she left, Blanche had told people I'd been feeling poorly, and hadn't been able to come to town. She'd told them I'd decided to lay off farming for a while because of my health—she hadn't told anybody about her birthday present except her brother Bailey Carlisle as it turned out. She must have been embarrassed or something I guess. I'd thought she would have bragged to the whole town about it, but no. Well, after that I didn't feel much like hanging around, so after I'd arranged for Otho's boy to leave groceries on my stoop once a week I just came on home and let them all think what they wanted.

I still didn't feel right, though, and when Moose Zacham came over along about noon to borrow some tackle for ploughing, I blurted the whole thing out to him, about the vacation and how I hadn't been sick at all. Moose is a good man, but he's none too bright, so I didn't go into my reasons. Anyway, he said, "I wouldn't want to take sides, Louis—seems to me you're both partly in the wrong." I started to explain that there hadn't been any quarrel, but then I thought there'd be no point in it, so I just said, "I wasn't asking you to take sides, Moose." Of course, the time was coming when I'd be hoping he would take sides.

That evening I had another visitor, Bailey Carlisle. He's a queer sort. Since his Hilda died some ten years back he practically never sets foot outside his hotel. He always was retiring—a little dried-up fish of a man. Well, he keeps to that hotel—where Blanche and Howard are staying now—but at the same time he has his nose in everybody's business. We used to have Sunday dinner at the hotel with him. He'd sit at the head of the table smiling and looking down like some proper old lady. And he'd finagle every bit of gossip he could out of us. He'd cluck and shake his head at the wild doings of the youngsters nowadays, but he always wanted to hear more.

Like I say, he came to visit me—I don't think he'd set foot in our house twice since we'd been married. He was polite and dainty, but he was nervous too. It seems Blanche had told him the truth she hadn't dared tell anybody else. And he was worried. "I felt I ought to offer you some advice," he said. "And whether you take it is your concern" (of course, he damn well thought it was *his* concern). He said, "I really think a month ought to be enough, Louis, I really do. A month would be wonderful, and I know Blanche and Howard would just love it. But much more—well, I have to say it's bound to look peculiar to people, they're bound to think things." He had the nerve to say, "Now I have a pretty good idea of your financial situation, and I know something about managing money, and even if you had twice as much as you do, I'd call what you aim to do extravagant, I really would—extravagant or even worse, Louis."

He didn't make me mad, though. I told him I'd think over what he had to say (though I really didn't think it was worth a second thought), and I even thanked him for his interest. And I knew that he did want to help, the poor thing, at least part of him did, because he was so lonesome.

We talked a while more, and then he said he ought to get back. He'd come in his car—he never walks anywhere if he can help it. I stood outside in the dark and watched his lights go down the hill through the trees, and then turn back up toward town. The wind was toward me—I could hear him a long time, till he went down behind the hill that's just this side of the city limits. Then I looked around me, and I realized that I was finally on my own. There was a full moon—it felt like clean water on me. "Well, sir . . ." I said, but then I didn't say anything else. It was the last day of March. I went to the barn and put out some fodder for the cow—she woke up and looked at me, and then went back to sleep—and I threw out some grain in the chicken yard. Then I rolled me up an old army blanket and went to the woods.

It was a warm night, so I had myself a swim in that lake I'd been thinking about. Then I went back up to the flat rocks, where I could hear the stream. I made myself a bed of leaves, and lay down and wrapped my blanket around me. Somehow I didn't feel sleepy, so I just lay there quiet as could be. I watched the night birds, and toward morning I saw a pair of weasels come for a drink of water. I thought about a lot of things that night, an awful lot of things. I thought about Blanche and me, how we'd just about stopped even having to think about each other—and how, now that Howard was almost grown, people expected us just to stand back and keep quiet and not do anything more—and I guess that's really what Blanche wanted, too. I thought about how all my life I'd always done what people expected. I knew they liked me for it, but I also knew that, when I thought about the way I'd lived, I had to smile sometimes, the way I smiled over Blanche and Howard—because I seemed like no more than a good little frisky pup.

I thought I'd be getting a letter from Blanche the next day, and I knew what she'd say. Before too long I'd get a picture postcard of Nashville from Howard; he'd tell me all about what he'd seen that I'd never seen, thinking I wanted to hear it or that it made any difference, thinking he'd done something important just because he'd been able to send that card. And too, I knew the things he wouldn't tell me because he didn't know they didn't make any difference either—the scrapes and fixes he'd have got into because he was just a country rube. I felt pretty sure that neither of them, Blanche or Howard, would do much more with my gift than what they'd already done—buy some things and then run off somewhere—there was nothing I could do to help them except go about my business, and maybe they'd understand a little more, watching me. Maybe they'd see that I was getting ready to . . . that I had my eye on the time when I was going to die. Maybe too they'd see that after all I didn't take much stock in heaven or what have you—and maybe then they'd realize that deep down they didn't either. If I'd had them there with me then, I could have told them some of what I had in my mind, maybe I could. I'd have liked to have hugged them to me in the woods there and talked to them about the way my mind was going. Well, there was nothing I could do about that, so I set myself to thinking about other things.

In the darkest part of the night, along about three or so, just before it started to get light, it seemed like I had a sort of vision or an inspiration that told me what it was I wanted to do with my time. It might have been a dream, but I really think I was awake, because I remember I saw the weasels afterwards. I'd been thinking I ought to build something, but I really didn't want to build a house like Henry David Thoreau's, because I didn't want to copy anything. I was lying on my back, then, looking up at the sky. It was a clear night, but there were tree branches criss-crossing over my head and hiding some of the stars. All of a sudden I realized I couldn't find the Big Dipper, or anything else I knew—I must have been drowsy, and maybe I'd got turned around so I didn't know which direction I was lying in. Well, while I was trying to find the Big Dipper I had my vision—I don't exactly know how to say it, but it was something like this: every star had a line going from it to every other star, so that the whole sky was full of millions of letters. And then it came to me that what I'd make would be a statue of a word, a special word. I remember it was when I saw the weasels that I knew how to find this word. It was a complicated idea, and I wonder how I thought of it like that—but I did. It seemed kind of a miracle. I remember I said to myself, "Louis, you've found yourself something worthy!" Of course the real miracle was still to come.

III

When I'd gone swimming in the lake I'd noticed that near the middle there was a spur of granite and limestone some ten yards long and five feet wide, just below the water. I decided I'd build the statue there.

I guess the way to find the word came to me because I'd been listening to the creek and the animals and so forth. I figured out that every place in the world has its own special sounds that you'll hear if you're there. Now, of course, there are lots of sounds you can hear in more than one place. But it seemed to me that the whole combination of sounds you hear somewhere must be peculiar to that one place. And I thought I'd have done something if I could make a statue of that kind of a combination. Maybe I was mistaken, I'm not sure. What you'd hear would depend on when you were listening, too — you'd have to choose your time.

I built up the spur of rock with gravel and cement till it was well above water level, for the base of my statue. I had this done by the end of April, so I decided to spend May and June discovering the word, and then when I built it I could write on it "May and June," and the year. During May I stayed at the lake during the day and slept home at night, and in June, when it was warmer, I did the reverse — because I wanted to get the night sounds as well as the day ones. I wrote down every sound I heard on a tablet I'd got for the purpose. I wrote not only the sounds animals and birds and insects made, but also those of the wind and the water, and the trees, and the rain (I sat out in it, with my tablet protected by Blanche's breadbox) and everything else. I write a fine hand, but by the end of June the tablet was full and I had written some on the inside cover.

I didn't write down any sound more than three times in a day, no matter how often I heard it, so I had a good deal of spare time. I answered the letters I got from Blanche and Howard, and thought, and just rested. The two months passed faster than you'd think.

I spent the first two days of July figuring out what the word was. I decided it would have two syllables, since that was the average number; so then I made all the words into two-syllable ones. I just stretched out the shorter ones — for instance there was a sound a little water beetle made when it took off flying, that was *tiss*, and I made that into *ti-iss*. In the same way I squeezed down the ones longer than two syllables when I could, and if I couldn't I just cut off part of them and kept the part I thought was most important. From *whip-poor-will*, for instance, I kept *poor-will*, because it made more sense than *whip-poor* would. So then I had everything changed into two-syllable words, written out in a new tablet. Then I started counting. I didn't want to find it out all together, so I did the first syllable by itself first. I'd figured out ahead of time how it should be done.

The middle sound or vowel was easy. I just had to count which sound came up most often. It turned out to be *oo* like in *moo*. The outside parts or consonants were harder to do, because some of the syllables, like *spree*, might have as many as three consonants on one side, and none on the other. So I had to write them in a special way. If there weren't any, I wrote *000*. If there was one I wrote it two more times, and if there were two I stuck in a zero somewhere. So then I counted up the consonants the same way as the vowels, and I ended up with *0lloo00*. When I struck out the zeros I had *lloo*, and since I didn't see how you could say two l's together, I made it *Loo*. Well, then I figured out the second syllable of my word the same way as the first. It turned out to be *Iss*. I'd worked past midnight, and I must have gotten a little sleepy, because I didn't realize what had happened until I said it out loud: *Loo-iss*. It was my very own name, Louis! I almost fell off my chair. I shook my head, and said it again to make sure. And then I just sat back and smiled. It was a miracle. The combination of everything I'd heard from the middle of the pond for the two months was my name. I had to shake my head. I decided right then that, since it didn't matter how it was spelled, as long as it was the same word, the statue would be "Louis." I went outside and stood on the porch for a while, and then I went to sleep.

Well, maybe I shouldn't have done it, but first thing next morning I wrote a letter to Blanche and told her what had happened. She'd been saying she was about ready to come on back since she couldn't talk me into coming away, and I thought I ought to prepare her a little, so she wouldn't be too surprised. I thought about telling Howard too, but I thought he wouldn't understand anyway. When I went into town that morning to buy some nails, two or three people said I looked like the cat that had got the canary, and I guess I must have seemed pretty sly and perky—but I kept my secret. Jim Nisbett at the hardware store asked me if I was aiming to build a new barn with all those nails, and I just grinned. When I passed the hotel, I waved to Bailey Carlisle in his office. He was sitting at his desk, and he acted like he didn't see me, so I shrugged my shoulders and went on about my business. I wasn't about to let that little dried-up thing get on my nerves.

It took me most of July to get all the wood I figured to need chopped down, and the platform for the statue built and cemented to the rock. It was the hardest work I'd done in years. As soon as I fed the cow and chickens and made myself a lunch, I'd be down to the lake, and I wouldn't be home till sundown. I cut trees as close to the shoreline as possible so they'd fall straight into the water or roll down to it. Then I'd have to tackle them and swim them out to the rock. At first some of the animals were frightened away by all the activity, but I left food for them and after a while they got used to me and came back. And I was always careful not to cut any trees that had nests in them. It was hot as could be there in the middle of the lake with no shade, but then I could have me a swim whenever I wanted. When I got the base done it stood a little more than three feet above the water; it was a yard deep and twelve yards long—I'd expanded it out about a yard beyond each end of the rock. I figured then that the letters could be ten feet tall and a yard wide, with eighteen-inch spaces between them. I had drawn a picture of the statue to scale, and it looked fine, so I started building.

The *L* was easy—it only took me three days to get it up. I nailed the bottom part of it to the platform, and then I strengthened it from behind with a couple of struts running from the back of the platform to the middle of the upright part of the letter. The next letter, *O*, was a good deal harder to build. Almost all the logs I had were straight, so I had to make it out of a number of short pieces with mitered ends. It took ten pieces altogether. I cut and shaped them onshore, where I could handle the wood better, but I decided to nail it together out on the platform, since I didn't think it would stand much rough handling. I built it section by section from the bottom up, attaching struts as I went along. I brought the stepladder down from the house because I knew I'd need it for the top part. It was the second week in August and I'd done the bottom half of the *O* already. It was near sundown, and I was getting ready to stop for the day, when the birds over on the shore started screaming and flying away. Then I saw the bushes thrashing, and then Howard came through. He looked like a city slicker in the picture show. He had on a cream-colored suit and a straw hat, and he was smoking a big cigar, grinning and waving to beat the band. It took me a minute to even figure out who he was.

IV

He claimed he'd just gotten tired of the city life and was a little home-sick. But it turned out later that he'd had two other reasons for coming back: he'd let some gal talk him into running through three quarters of his money already, and then Blanche had been writing him saying she was worried about me, and that she wanted him home when she got here. She'd even got Bailey Carlisle to write him, I later found out. But he didn't tell me any of that. The first time I suspected something was when I told him Blanche would be home in a couple of days, and he acted real surprised but he was blushing at the same time. I let it go.

All through supper he told me about what he'd seen and done—I thought he'd never stop. He kept that straw hat on till I told him he didn't need it in the house. In a while he said, "How's Uncle Bailey been doing?" and I said I couldn't say, since I hadn't seen him. I guess that sort of set Howard off. "Now Daddy," he said, "now what the hell is it you're building down there in the woods?" I studied a while before I said any-thing. Maybe it was wrong for me not to tell him the truth, I don't know. For one thing I wanted to make it as easy on him as I could—I figured he'd have a hard enough time understanding what I did tell him. "Well sir," I said, "I'm building a statue of my name." And then I said, "Son, while you were a boy I made it my business to explain my doings to you, because you depended on me—because you couldn't understand any other way. Now you're grown up I'll give you whatever advice you want. But I won't justify myself any more. Why should I? Especially not during our vacation." I'm not sure he understood that—he sort of shrugged and nodded and went off to bed.

Well, for the next two or three days it was raining and what with one thing and another I didn't get to the woods. I'd let the house get into a mess, so I spent most of the time straightening it up so it wouldn't be so bad for Blanche when she got here. She was so happy to see me that we hardly talked about anything until the day after she arrived. But then she started in. I remember she said, "Now heavens above, what do you want to go doing that to your name for, Louis? Your name was just fine without you putting up any statue of it!" I did explain to her again that it wasn't just a statue of my name, but she wouldn't listen to reason. I even showed her my tablets, but she said, "I don't care about all that, it's still your name, and every time I talk to you I'll have to think about that blasted lake! I think you're going to *ruin* your name, Louis, is what I think you're going to do. Why, what if the neighbors saw it while they were out hunting or something?" I tried to argue with her but she would just say, "I don't know how I can hold up my head if you keep on." I told her she was working her own self up but it didn't do any good so finally I said I'd hold off for a week. Of course I was disappointed in her, but I tried not to let her see it.

She brightened up. Almost every day she would flounce Howard and me into town to show everybody that we were back to normal. She wouldn't even let Howard wear his new hat and suit. He and I would sit and talk to some of the other men while she did her shopping or went to the beauty parlor. It was funny: I really did enjoy seeing my friends again, even though I hadn't missed them at all in the woods—particularly my neighbor Moose Zacham, because he so clearly was relieved to see that everything was all right. The one thing I could hardly stand was dinner at the hotel. I'd never seen Bailey Carlisle simper and smirk so. He nearly patted me on the head. And he served us the best meal we'd ever had there.

I admit it was partly because I was put out so by Bailey Carlisle that I went straight back to work on the statue first thing the next morning before Blanche and Howard were awake. About noon Blanche came running down to the lake white as a sheet. It was the first time she'd been there. I was up on the stepladder working on the top part of the O. I think the letters must have been even larger than she'd expected, because she stopped short, and just looked for a minute. Then she ran down to the shore and started saying something and beckoning for me to come in. When I yelled out "What do you want?" she put her finger to her lips and said, "Shh," and stamped her foot for me to be quiet. So I swam on in.

She had seen Moose and some others walking down to the woods to go hunting, and she was afraid they'd catch me at work on the statue. I told her then that I aimed to go on with it, and she might as well reconcile herself to it. I told her she was letting it get all out of proportion. Besides, I said, if people thought it was peculiar it looked to me like it was her place to side with me and not with them. I told her I knew she might not understand it, but the important thing was, it was something I'd made up my mind to do. "Blanche," I said, "I've never done anything like this before, and I'll never again, if it's any consolation to you. Besides," I said, "they probably won't be hunting in this part of the woods anyway."

She said, "It's just crazy, Louis, crazy," and I told her no it wasn't.

She said, "Louis, Louis, think about me!"

I said, "I do think about you, don't you know that? I'm thinking about you this very second," but I didn't tell her what I was thinking. I was thinking how silly and pretty she seemed—younger than she had in years. She saw how I was looking at her, and she sort of blushed. I said, "Now you go on back to the house, Blanche, and don't you worry, little thing." I thought she was about to cry, so I kissed her and sent her off. I could tell by the way she stomped away that she was still angry.

I'd hoped to get the O done that day, so I kept working till it was too dark to see. I didn't quite finish it, but there was nothing to do but go on home. I thought it was odd that, when I got near the house, I didn't see any light. I found a note from Blanche on the table—she said she and Howard had gone in to town to spend the night at the hotel because Bailey Carlisle had taken sick, and they wanted me to come as soon as I could. Well, I took the lantern and set out, but I hadn't gone very far when two ideas came to me: first, that there was a good chance that Bailey wasn't really sick at all, but that they just wanted to distract me from my project, and, second, that with the very lantern I had in my hand I could finish up the O that night, like I'd wanted to. I thought about it for a minute, and then I made up my mind. I cut back across the northeast corner of Moose Zacham's land into the woods. Since I knew my way I put out the lantern to save kerosene—I realized it was low. It occurs to me that if I only hadn't put it out they would have seen me coming back, and nothing would have happened. Because they weren't at the hotel at all. They were hiding some place where they could watch the house—maybe they were in the barn, they might even have been at the Zachams'.

I got the O finished pretty quickly. I was tired, though—I'd worked hard—and something seemed to tell me to stick close to my statue that night. It was warm but so cloudy it looked like we might have a shower, so I put out the lantern again and crawled under the platform where I could keep pretty dry. I fell right to sleep—this must have been about 11:30 or so.

The next thing I remember is feeling something dripping on my hand—I guess at first I thought it had started raining. I was confused, and still half asleep. I smelled kerosene, but I thought it was just the lantern, and I remember I reached over to make sure I hadn't knocked it over. But my hand was stinging, and I realized I'd got kerosene on it somehow. Then, clear as could be, I heard Blanche's voice saying "Be careful." I must have thought I was dreaming. But then I heard it again—it came from the shore, and she was yelling, "Now be careful!" I turned over, and then I heard Howard's voice coming from directly over me saying, "God damn it! There's some kind of animal crawled up under here!" Then I heard a splash (it was Howard jumping into the water) and then the whole place lit up.

V

What can I say? I don't want it to sound like they were worse than they really were. After all, they didn't know what they were doing—they didn't know I was under there, and then for all my explaining they still didn't know what the statue was. In a way, they hadn't grown up. I've forgiven them in my heart, but no one's forgiven me.

I remember the first thing I did was to look out across the water. The light was so bright I could see everything. There was Howard splashing away—he always did swim like he was about to drown—and there on the shore were Blanche and Bailey Carlisle. Finally I saw what had happened. I peeped up between the logs of the platform, and I saw the L and the O that were standing over me all on fire. Howard had poured kerosene over them and set them on fire. There was nothing I could do to save them. A breeze had come up that whipped out long streamers of fire out behind the letters. Somehow it looked real fine, even though I did almost feel like crying. I remember I thought I wished I could have got the whole thing done before they burnt it, because it would have been a real fine sight.

Just as I started to crawl out, the fire jumped down and blocked my way. Howard had put most of the kerosene on the letters, but he had poured some over the platform itself, and some had dripped down through, so that there was fire every place I could have moved. Even though we'd had some rain during the summer, the wood had pretty much dried out sitting there in the sun day after day, so that it was burning fast. I know I'd have suffocated if it hadn't been for the breeze to carry the smoke away. When I could I looked across the lake again. I saw that the three of them were leaving. Even if I had felt like calling to them, they couldn't have heard me over the roar of the fire.

There was nothing I could do, so I got into a position where I could watch the letters burn, and waited. My clothes kept catching on fire but I managed to put them out. My hand that the kerosene had dripped over got burned—I've just lately been able to use it again. I lay there thinking I was probably going to burn to death before it was over. Like they say it does, my life went through my head, and I remember it was then that I began to get angry. I started trying to kick loose the platform from over me. The letters were about to fall anyway, and my kicking brought them down. Parts of them fell in the water, and other parts onto the platform over me, and the burning ash came sifting down through the logs. Then I started screaming, "Help! Help!" and then finally I guess I passed out. When I came to again it was pouring rain, and the fire was out. It was the rain that saved me.

I think I must have fallen asleep or lost consciousness several more times before I got myself free, just before dawn. I rested a while, and then I swam to the shore and started walking. I had to go slow because I was burned and so tired. It must have been about six o'clock when I got to town. I walked through and started at the other end and worked my way back. I went to every house. I went to the door, and when they opened it, I said, "Look at me, look at what my family's done to me. My Blanche and my Howard did it, and that Bailey Carlisle." I was streaked black from the soot, my clothes were half burnt off, my face was blistered, my hair was frizzled up. I held out my burned hand so they could see it.

Some of them said, "Louis, come on in here and let us fix you up," but I kept on. Lucy Patterson's little girl screamed and hid when she saw me, and Lucy said, "What are you saying, Louis? Why Blanche was out half the night, worried sick." All I said to her was, "They did this to me. What can a man do when his own family treats him so." I remember she said, "You should be ashamed of yourself, Louis," and slammed her door in my face. Maybe that should have warned me I was making a mistake, but it only made me madder. Before I was half through town there was a group of people following me—some of them laughing, some telling me to stop. A lot of them were youngsters. I didn't pay them any attention. But they were making a good deal of noise.

I was walking up to the hotel when the door opened and Blanche stepped out to see what was happening. She took one look at me and fainted right there. The people following me stopped talking. Howard and Bailey Carlisle were close behind Blanche. I didn't move till Howard had seen that she was all right, and then I started saying my piece, pointing at the three of them. Howard was red as a beet—he was bending over and pretending to pat Blanche's cheeck, so he'd have something to do, and so he could hide his face. But Blanche had waked up, and she was looking me straight in the eye. I've never seen her so angry. I shook my finger at them, and I said, "Look at them. They did this to me." That Bailey Carlisle, he listened for a minute, and then he just walked back into the hotel and closed the door, leaving Blanche and Howard out on the porch by themselves. You might know he'd do something of the kind.

I imagine somebody had run ahead to tell Claude Witherspoon our sheriff, because he was waiting for me. He told me he didn't want to, but he'd have to arrest me for disturbing the peace if I didn't calm down. I said I had two more houses to go, and then I'd be done, so if he aimed to arrest me he'd better do it (I'd gotten a little carried away by then). He said, "It's not right, Louis, for a man to treat his family this way. It's shameful, Louis, and you'll be sorry for it." I said, "I may be—but what's shameful, Claude, is the way they burnt my statue," but he didn't answer me. He just stood aside and let me go on. The last house was widow Thomas's—she's old and simple-minded. She was out on her porch, and I remember after I'd said my piece she burst out laughing, and then she stopped and she clapped her hands and said, "Go on, get out of here! Get! Shoo! Get away from here!" I guess I remember that because those were the last words anybody said to me.

I had intended to stop and do my speech at the Zachams' but by the time I got there I was so worn out I just went on home. "Well," I said to myself, "I guess they got more than they bargained for, didn't they? If they hadn't been so concerned about people talking, everything would have been fine. Okay then: I've given people something to talk about for sure." Then I dressed my hand and went to sleep. It seemed to me that I'd got everything worked out.

Things didn't happen the way I expected though. I thought people would be coming to commiserate with me and bring me food and so forth, so I waited mostly in bed for two or three days, but nobody came. Finally I walked over the the Zachams'. It was Sunday, and they'd just come back from church. They were sitting on the porch. When they saw me coming Alice said something to Moose and then she went inside. Moose sat there, but he looked real solemn and sad. I could practically read his mind. I didn't have to go through with it—I already knew what he'd say to me. I knew he'd say he couldn't ask me in. It came to me then that people had set their hearts against me, and not against Blanche and

Howard and Bailey Carlisle. Of course it made me feel bad, but when I saw poor old Moose in such a predicament, scratching his head and trying to figure out what he ought to do, I couldn't help chuckling to myself. So I just tipped my hat to him and kept going, like I was out for a walk and not coming to see them at all. I've kept away from them since then. I don't want to put old Moose on the spot. I can't resist crossing his land though now and again when he's out in the fields, just to see what he'll do. He always manages not to notice me.

For a while I did have some fun with the people in the stores and so on when I'd go into town. I'd speak to them and when they'd look down and not answer I'd say something like "Cat got your tongue?" I got sick of it, though, after a while. Then I started explaining and apologizing to them, and taking all the blame on myself. I told them I'd been crazy and perverse even to think of building the statue. I said I'd been selfish and thoughtless—I told them anything I could think of, but still they looked away and pretended not to hear me. Part of the trouble was that they always looked so serious and angry I couldn't help laughing, even when I was apologizing. Now I've left off talking to them. I tried staying home all the time, but it got to be too lonesome, so now almost every day I go in and sit outside the courthouse so I can listen to people talking.

Like I say, I haven't talked to my family at all. They stay at the hotel, and it looks to me like they don't come out much more than Bailey Carlisle. There are a number of things I'd like to find out about them. I wonder, for instance, how they get along with the townspeople. I wonder whether Blanche feels disgraced—whether she feels she can "hold up her head." And then I'd like to know exactly what they had planned the night of the fire. It's pretty clear that Bailey Carlisle was only shamming sick. But I wonder what would have happened if I'd gone on to the hotel. Did they have somebody there to keep me occupied till they burnt the statue? And then I wonder too whether or not they would have admitted doing it. Maybe they would have claimed to have been at the doctor's, and not to know anything about it. Or maybe they would have said they did it for my own benefit. Either way it would have been a good show.

The way I see it now is this. Most of the people never will forgive me, no matter what happens. But supposing Blanche and I get back together, things might ease up a little anyway. So the main question is Blanche— Howard will do anything the both of us tell him. Bailey Carlisle has probably advised Blanche never to have anything to do with me again, but I give her credit for having more sense than to take too much stock in what he says. So it depends on Blanche and me.

Now I've thought about writing her and telling her to come on back, and I expect she'd do it. On the other hand, it seems to me that it's her place to make the first move, so I've been waiting to see if she will. In fact I've decided I won't do anything till the end of the vacation. If she decides to come back before then, she can. If not, maybe I'll write her after the vacation, and then again I might not, I can't say. It might be that she's waiting for the year to be over too, I don't know. I'd thought about building the statue again, and sometimes I walk down to look at the lake; but I couldn't see much point in making a second try at it. I wonder if Blanche thinks I'm building it again. Anyway, what I have to do now is to get through the winter somehow, and get to the end of the vacation. And, like I told Blanche at the beginning, we won't know what it is till it's over. Whatever happens, I think that in the deepest part of my heart I'll be more proud than sorry, even if I'm lonely the rest of my days. I wouldn't tell anybody else, but I have to tell it to myself.

But sometimes I do miss my friends so much I wish we'd never taken the vacation—and so maybe before it's over I'll be able to apologize and not even smile at them.

NADINE,
THE SUPERMARKET,
THE STORY ENDS

GROWING UP in the beautiful lonesome Cumberland Mountains, Nadine Florence might almost as well have had no family at all. She gave herself over to solitary speculation or spent time following the progress of the seasons. On her sixteenth birthday she saw the famous moonbow of the Cumberland Falls. The wooden boardwalk led behind the falling water. Nadine was scared because she didn't want to die there in the mountains and yet she didn't know where she ought to go. But she was brave too.

Nadine was average height, pretty, a bit on the thin side the way mountaineers are, fair with light hair. She made people feel more peaceful. She stole a page out of an atlas so she could keep track of her wanderings, and set out hitchhiking. First she headed south into Tennessee. The mountains were grander, the people seemed weaker and more cunning. There were lots of times when pretty young boys, bull-necked men, or feeble codgers tried to take advantage, but Nadine's earnest mildness always turned away violence. She might work as a waitress, cook, or dishwasher in the truck stops to keep and clothe herself, save some money and then move on.

Nadine's head wasn't as full of rubbish as most young girls' are. She bought a diary and wrote down things she wanted to remember. She wrote, "The third look preserves me. That's when they see I'm a pretty little thing. But first they don't see me at all and then they see I'm a stranger." Nadine knew the second look was dangerous. In its dawning she'd watched herself dismembered in people's minds. She also made cheerful diary entries about how what she'd learned in school was coming in handy.

She stayed in one Tennessee village for half a year, liked it so much she thought she might settle. She boarded with and worked for an old lady who ran the beauty parlor. The lady called herself Mlle. Renée. In her salon was a picture of Mauna Loa. Nadine began as a manicurist but soon by dint of studying magazines and watching Mlle. Renée she became a hairdresser and all-round beautician. When she parted a customer's black or brown or red or blonde hair and saw the grey scalp she would think of the grey skull bone beneath, and of the grey brain matter beneath that.

During her spare hours Nadine was usually alone. Sitting at the window or before the dresser in her attic room she took to making up stories. As she thought of them she wrote them in a bound accounting book from the dimestore. It was enjoyable but not easy. She wrote her stories very slowly and often returned to change what happened in them.

Mlle. Renée's customers liked Nadine because, as they said, "She does a real good job, she's friendly and she knows how to keep her mouth shut." Mlle. Renée considered retiring and turning the business over to Nadine. Finally she said, "I'd like to make you my partner because I'm getting on in years. And then if it works you can take over entirely. I think you have promise. I could never sell nail polish before you came." Nadine thanked her for her kindness but asked for time to decide, making it scrupulously clear she might refuse. Mlle. Renée was a squat spinster with coarse swarthy skin and flashing black eyes. When Nadine left she said, "And don't try opening your own salon here, either. That trick won't work."

Nadine headed northeast into North Carolina where she met Michael Standish, a policeman who said, "May I help you, Miss?" when he saw her in the square searching for a restaurant. He was full of rich dark color in his hair and eyes and skin, the way mountaineers never are. That night he and Nadine fell in love jitterbugging. Neither was ready to marry so they decided to drive away together. Michael said goodbye to his uniform a little ruefully. They kissed and kissed in the car, registered as Mr. and Mrs. Standish in a motel and with no light but the moon in the window and a TV lamp they made love till dawn. Nadine had no basis for comparison or she would have realized that Michael was almost inhumanly gentle. They said, "I love you, I love you" the whole night. When she thought back on it she always remembered his damp hair.

They kept traveling—Michael couldn't afford to be caught in an illicit relationship if he ever wanted to return to the force. Sometimes they picked up hitchhikers. They drove into Virginia and then Nadine said, "I'm homesick for Kentucky," so they turned west. It was midwinter. At Hazard Nadine wrote her name on a slip of paper and sealed it in a bottle.

She tramped through the snowy woods to a protected crevice in an outcropping of rock, and she left the bottle there. It reminded her of the condoms Michael flushed down the toilet or flung from the car into the snow wherever they went.

Finally they came to rest in a large apartment in a Louisville slum. They warmed bowls of canned spaghetti on the radiator and talked about finding jobs. Suddenly they realized they were ready for marriage. Nadine was eighteen, Michael twenty-one. They found jobs, married, started saving money. Michael said they ought to move soon because the black slum was only a block away and advancing. They moved, and moved again, each time into a better neighborhood. Nadine wrote in her diary, "I do miss those old women with newspapers tied around their feet. Some day I may dress that way." Michael saw this when he was snooping among Nadine's belongings and teased her about it.

Nadine said, "Why should you snoop? Is it what you learn as a policeman?" Michael said, "I believe you're ashamed of writing such foolishness, honey." "Your snooping is the point," said Nadine, "and I don't know why you can't think of some other line of work. It makes me uneasy to be on either side of the law. You're too good for it, Michael." "Why didn't you tell me this before?" said Michael. Nadine said, "Let's go to bed and love each other." Michael said, "You were cruel to say that about those women. And if you don't want me to snoop you shouldn't be secretive. We're married, for better or worse. I don't keep secrets from you, do I? It isn't fair." "It wasn't really a secret," Nadine said, "not from you, not yet anyway." Michael said, "You're right, let's go to bed and stop this silly quarrel." "I'm sorry, I don't want to any more now," said Nadine. "You're right," Michael said, "I don't want to either."

Their marriage ended. At first as a distraction and then for its own sake Nadine studied American history and political science at the University of Kentucky in Lexington. She especially enjoyed the history of the early decades of the country, of the pilgrims struggling together at Plymouth and of the settlers and explorers in Kentucky. With a scholarship and two jobs she managed but she never had enough time for schoolwork. She had neither time nor, after Michael, much interest for the youngsters who flirted with her. But since she was curious to see how Lexington's wealthy lived in their green white-fenced farms she accepted an invitation to a ball, and there she met Gordon Crichter who was to be her second husband. He courted Nadine so imaginatively that she didn't know whether or not he loved her. He was twelve years older than she, a Korean War veteran, rich, ambitious and deceptive. He said, "I love you, Nadine. Please be my wife, I'll always love you." Nadine wrote in her diary, "What use does he have for me? What do I want?" Gordon said, "I'll make you happier than you've ever been. Say yes, we'll honeymoon in Europe." Nadine wrote, "Be kind." She said, "My friend, let's get hitched."

Nadine listened to Gordon talk about horses, people, his family, furniture, the stock market, sailing, shoes. She didn't yet talk about what was important to her because she didn't yet know how. She went to journalism school during the day while Gordon was at his office. Through his influence she wrote human interest stories for local newspapers. In ten years she and Gordon had three children. One was autistic, the other two lovely, especially the daughter. Through them Nadine became acquainted with a wide loose group of other parents, and found a few lifelong friends. She learned to make small talk and also to make speeches at civic meetings. Gordon grew more sentimental. He enjoyed referring to his rich full life and would say, "We've been lucky, Nadine, in spite of our ups and downs."

Gordon's aunts and uncles died, his companies merged and spawned. Nadine handled the charitable donations. Giving away money was a little like writing her stories: it could be taken lightly but the more seriously she took it the more difficult and even painful and yet exciting it grew. She and Gordon disagreed. He wanted the money to go to art museums and parks and she wanted it to go to medical research or famine relief. He threw up his hands: "Do what you like, it's only money." Nadine changed her mind from year to year. Sometimes she thought educational television was the only answer and bestowed large sums accordingly. If only she could have handed over sacks and bushels of cash or, better, gold or, better, food or medicines or whatever. Instead she signed a slip of paper and sealed it in a paper envelope and as a result sometimes a fatigue weighed on her. One of her children might ask, "Mummy, are you feeling old?" "Not young," Nadine would say.

She felt especially not young with the mumps she caught from her daughter. In her fever she raved, "What have I done with my time?" Upon recovery she seemed in a new and somewhat schizoid relation to humanity in general. As if "the people" had become at once her arch enemy and only charge.

Immediately she threw herself back into journalism and wrote moving forceful articles about women's rights and kindness. Her reputation grew. She became editor of one of the newspapers she wrote for. Most of Gordon's family, having ignored and tolerated her, now actively opposed her. Gordon's father said, "Really, you ought to curtail this. She's making a spectacle of herself. She's starting to crusade. Seriously, Gordon." Gordon made suggestions but Nadine stuck to her guns and he acquiesced. They were sitting in her bedroom. Rubbing his chin he watched her and said, "Let them be embarrassed. You're what matters. Who'd believe that at this late date I'm being educated by my own dear wife. Who'd have supposed you could still surprise me." Nadine said, "You surprise me too. And you do make me happy." "I know why," said Gordon. Nadine looked at his tan handsome face, at the canopied bed, at the corner of a coat protruding from the closet, at the bookcase, out the windows down the terraced lawn at the horses grazing. Gordon said, "It's because I applaud when you side-step the traps I lay for you."

Writing editorials inevitably brought Nadine into politics. Gordon had long wielded considerable influence with a certain graceful negligence, but Nadine had to be careful. She wrote in her journal, "I may as well try my hand though." She began to take stands on issues and endorse candidates. Her main advantage was that she herself was exploring, was never quite sure what she was up to, so that nobody could second-guess her. The public often disregarded her appeals but her success was phenomenal. Whether or not they followed her the people admired her patent integrity. It was inexhaustibly refreshing to them.

Party bosses tried bribes and then threats of financial and finally bodily harm, to no avail, and then gave Nadine a seat on the state committee. At this point Nadine realized that her political power was starting to snowball. "I'll ride it out," she said. She was more than a little frightened. "Now or never," she said. She burnt all her journals and notebooks, all the stories she had written.

Meanwhile people had been calculating and conferring and now they asked Nadine to run for U.S. Senate and she accepted the nomination. It was unheard-of, it took people's breath away. It was discussed in an article in the *Wall Street Journal*. Nadine won by a narrow margin. She hadn't even done much campaigning—the machine had supported her with posters near every polling place in the state.

She drove to Louisville alone. The city seemed quiet in a smoky dusk. As she penetrated the slum pedestrians stared at her car. It was November and under a reddish moon neon liquor and pawn shop signs were tangled. She stopped and looked up at the apartment she had shared with Michael. In the window a drunk or drugged black slouched toying with a knife. Above, large as the whole apartment, Nadine saw her own grave face on a billboard. Later when she reentered the freeway she was amazed and heartened by the orderliness of the traffic. It was easy to imagine a less rational, more violent race. She said, "They deserve better." She decided that her senatorial tenure would be revolutionary in its way. It was raining. Lights danced and the water was blown to the sides off her windshield. She decided to spend much of her time at an office in Kentucky, and to be in Washington only when necessary.

From here on her history is a matter of public record—the positions she took, how she voted, her committee work, her famous speeches that left increasing portions of the country surprised and convinced, and then the deadlocked convention on which like an inspiration fell the idea of nominating Nadine for president. "This is the big time," she said. She felt as if she were becoming exoskeletal. Busy as she was, she managed to do her own hair every night, perhaps watching herself on the late news. Gordon traveled with her some but more often she was alone and it was then she would wake in the early morning and feel certain she was doing right.

Her opponent didn't exert himself at first but halfway through the campaign when polls showed her closing the gap he set to work in earnest. On national television Mlle. Renée, toothless but still vigorous, claimed Nadine had been a bad egg from the beginning, and hinted at embezzling in the beauty shop. Nadine's first husband Michael was discovered in Oklahoma happily married, owner and manager of a motel. He withstood and then revealed the opposition's attempts to bribe him to speak out against Nadine. She watched him being interviewed and saying nothing on television. He looked handsome and negligible. A wife and children hovered out of focus in the background. All the time Nadine felt herself becoming public property and growing vacant with nothing but will and principle and kindness left in her. On election day she seemed essentially a name printed on millions and millions of paper ballots marked in secret and dropped into boxes across the nation. She slept and awoke the first woman president of the United States. It was a kind of disaster for Nadine. It was a kind of triumph for the people.

Now I'd like to tell a true story. It's about myself and it happened recently. My husband Bob had gone to work and I'd driven Priscilla and little Gavin to school. When I came back I noticed that some of our daffodils had started to bloom. Bob and I enjoy gardening. Our lawn is one of the prettiest in Verdant Park. Verdant Park is a pretty suburb of Lexington, Kentucky. We have a grade school, several churches, a shopping center, shady streets, smooth lawns, tidy houses. Bob has a twenty-minute drive to work in downtown Lexington.

I picked up the kitchen and had a second cup of coffee in the breakfast nook. Robins were finding worms near where our lawn meets the Smiths' and the Smiths' Irish setter on its long leash chased them. The colors were brilliant because of the overcast sky. The Smiths are older, he's an orthodontist. They have a son, Frank, in junior high. We don't know them well. I enjoy the time just after Bob and the children have left in the morning. I write memoranda then. I noticed that the detergent rash under my wedding ring was angrier and was spreading to adjacent fingers.

In the bathroom I brushed my teeth. I washed my face and stood before the mirror to examine it in the mixed sunlight and flourescent light. I put on my makeup and arranged my hair.

The gravel in the drive crunched pleasantly under my tires. The streets of Verdant Park were smooth and empty — it seemed a mere formality to wait for the red light to be extinguished and the green to come on. In a month the streets would be full of children but now they were all at school. As I pulled into the shopping center parking lot I tooted and waved at a friend who was driving away. The developers must have expected Verdant Park to grow more rapidly than it has — I've never seen more than a quarter of the large parking lot in use. Today it was almost empty. Marcy Smith from next door seemed to be at the beauty salon — the lilac Chrysler parked there was hers, I supposed.

The market itself is large in proportion to the parking lot. In fact we have the largest supermarket of any Lexington suburb. I didn't bother to lock the car, the place seemed so deserted. Already the asphalt was warm. I had worn sunglasses and as I stepped onto the automatic door opener platform I shoved them onto the top of my head as if there were other eyes there in my hair which now needed protection from the flourescent panels covering the ceiling.

I always forget to bring a sweater when I come shopping and the air conditioning feels too chilly at first on my upper arms until in a while I cease to notice it. At first also I notice a whispering hum which I take to be the sound of the air conditioning and various refrigeration apparatus.

The door is on the side at the front corner. As I enter, ahead of me stretches the large open space between a row of check-out stands at my right and the store's plate glass front at my left. Signs painted onto this plate glass announce specials. From inside all of it is mirror-writing. I can read most of the words but the numbers in the prices are more difficult because a series of letters, say "chuck," is intelligible only in one direction, from the c to the k, whereas a series of numbers is intelligible in both directions — 89 as well as 98. Only one checker, a woman my age, stood among the registers. I pulled free a shopping cart with the distinctive whanging noise you hear only in supermarkets.

I idled fifteen minutes in the international corner, my foot hooked over the lower rack of my cart. It was remarkable, the odd things brought together here. Their only common feature was that they were foreign. I chose some Iranian flatbread for hors d'oeuvres and a Swiss chocolate bar. I remembered that the last time I'd had Swiss chocolate was on my honeymoon. I decided to nibble at it as I shopped.

The next section along the wall is for bread and other baked goods. The odor of these comes through their cellophane and plastic wrappers to make me feel safe and a little childish and hungry. I've often thought it would be delicious to fall onto a bed of soft loaves of bread. Today it occurred to me that this section felt comfortable for another reason. Suppose I were imprisoned in the building. I could easily get to the bread, cakes and doughnuts and also to the peanut butter and jellies in their jars in the adjacent tier. Whereas to someone without an opener the beautifully labelled cans elsewhere in the store might as well have contained ashes.

I didn't need anything in this section and I was passing by when a certain redness among the cakes caught my eye. I came closer and bent to examine it. Someone had written on each of a row of cake boxes with what seemed a deep true red lipstick. For the most part the writer had simply copied over the lettering on the label but on at least one package he had marked down the price by half. I swabbed at the writing with my finger and sniffed it. Definitely it was lipstick.

Just then a shopping cart moved in the next aisle. I felt certain the lipstick culprit was there escaping or doing damage. I ran to the end of my aisle, around the shelves and crashed my cart directly into one pushed by an elderly lady. She had been pushing her cart quietly because a baby was sleeping in it. The baby opened its eyes, shut them, and went back to sleep. The woman's face was angrily flushed. I apologized—explaining could only make matters worse. She hurried away out of sight. I stood shaking. What had come over me? I was embarrassed and yet, remembering the woman's expression I felt inclined to laugh. My heart was racing. I didn't move again until I was calmer.

Then I was moving through the aisles again, strolling idly, letting my thoughts wander. I hardly knew what I selected from the shelves during that quarter hour. I was shopping inefficiently, without a list and without traversing the entire store methodically aisle by aisle. Whenever something I needed popped into my head I'd simply locate it by consulting the signs hung from the ceiling, go directly to it and then wander until something else came to mind. Those signs are very helpful—in fact they are necessary now that supermarkets are becoming so large.

It occurred to me that my life is like being in a large supermarket, except that there are no signs to identify the various sections, so that I seem to wander through a maze of riches. But with my life as with our Verdant Park market I am seldom entirely lost. There is a certain general supermarket floorplan with which I am familiar. It must be almost as old as the supermarkets themselves. I and other shoppers know it though we don't understand much of its rationale. The signs are necessary because the layout of each particular store differs in an unpredictable way from the general plan. And anyway, I thought, as far as my life was concerned those signs suspended from the ceiling really were there after all, a hanging garden of signs.

I was at the beginning of the spice section where the salt and food coloring and cornstarch give way to cheaper brands of spices in tin boxes. Beyond these, in a section all to itself, is a more expensive brand in matching clear glass jars. There are some sixty different kinds. Each time I think of it I buy a new one. I've accumulated about thirty already. Today I chose anise.

I seemed to discover a bit of the supermarket rationale when, wheeling around, I noticed that in the facing tier were the various precious meats — smoked oysters, sardines, etc. in their own little tins and bottles. And further down that tier I saw more of the same: rows and rows of metal basket racks each containing a heap of jars of babyfood. How I had missed buying it as my children outgrew it! As I passed I stirred one of the bins with my hand to hear the jars click like jewelry.

All this made me remember I needed pickles. If packaging were the only determing factor they'd have been nearby. However as I happened to know they were at the other side of the store. Tears started in my eyes when I looked at their many quiet tart greens, and at how full the jars stood. I chose some sweet gherkins and olives stuffed with almonds.

The side and back walls of the store are lined with shelves up to a convenient height of about five and a half feet. Above, one sees featureless pale green plaster stucco. Why no windows? I wondered. Why not take advantage of the free daylight? Perhaps sunlight would damage the merchandise and also air-conditioned, lighted and windowless, the store can seem a timeless place, temperature and illumination the same at all hours and all seasons. Furthermore, I thought, the absence of windows and the long flourescent panels set into the ceiling permit all parts of the store to be uniformly lighted, so that one's groceries seem in a state of suspended animation until one wheels them out the door and all their colors change, gleams and shadows fall across them and one realizes how perishable they are.

On impulse I returned to the international section and bought some Chinese food, chow mein and noodles. The latter reminded me that I needed macaroni. It and the other pasta lay in plastic sacks like pillows or sandbags, piled and spilling over. In the same section lay other larger bags of lentils, rice, peas, beans, all dried. Nearby in colorful cardboard boxes were entire dehydrated dinners for four. Of course drying is a very old method of preservation but it seems to have grown much more common recently. There were, as I knew, elsewhere in the store boxes of dried mashed potatoes and jars of dried liquids such as coffee, skim milk and imitation orange juice.

Leaving these foods I paused at a plywood magazine stand. Since the store's customers are almost all women the magazines are almost all women's magazines. Along with the general ones there were special magazines or booklets for young mothers, dieters, brides, as well as instruction and pattern booklets for sewing, knitting and crocheting, and paperback cookbooks. Lying flat on the base of the stand were comic books for children arranged according to genre—western, comic animals, super people, horror, love, war.

The magazine rack was the first of the store's several sections of inedible merchandise. Next was a miscellaneous section with vitamins and aspirin and a few other patent medicines, bandages, cosmetics, razor blades, stationery and some kitchen hardware—knives and pancake turners mostly. Most of the items were affixed to cards hung from aluminum hooks. Next came detergents, bleaches, household cleaners, floor waxes, liquid plumbers and so forth. The last inedibles were rolls and boxes of paper, metal foil and polyethelene for wrapping or cleaning.

Then—it seemed almost a reward for having come through the preceding area—I found myself among fresh produce agreeably displayed in sloping waist-high bins. There were red, yellow, and green apples, all very glossy, stacked in pyramids, as were the grapefruits and oranges. We have such fruits almost year-round now. I don't know where they come from. An employee wearing the yellow supermarket uniform stood at the lettuce picking out those heads which had wilted and tossing them over her shoulder into a canvas garbage sack slung from a wheeled frame. The odor of celery was stronger than any other, and it seemed rather medicinal, perhaps because the white enamelled metal here evokes memories of hospitals.

Tomatoes were at my side. No longer piled in bins, these were packaged in oblong plastic four-tomato crates, the crates wrapped in cellophane. I suppose I'll grow accustomed to this system of merchandising in time but as yet I dislike it because the printing on top and the wadded cellophane beneath makes it difficult to know whether the tomatoes are good. Indeed, though I try to choose carefully, in the last such package I had bought two of the tomatoes had been rotten. I had meant to ask for a refund, but now I didn't wish to bother.

Ten yards away hung one, and further down the corridor another white metal scale for customers to weigh their own fruits and vegetables in. These scales consisted of wide scoop-shaped pans suspended under large dial faces. In the tray of one of them someone had left some bananas the ends of which stood up in a row like ancient teeth. The scales themselves looked like huge skulls or sculptures of skulls in the air above the bins—totems or idols, I thought, to ward mortality off the vegetables, perhaps by projecting it into the minds of customers like me. They seemed really rather cheery, swaying there.

Beyond the tomatoes the fruit began. Fat oranges with a brand name stamped onto the skin of each gave out their fragrance. They were stacked in pyramids as were, beyond, the lemons and next the soft-looking grapefruits and beyond them a fruit I didn't recognize which was spherical, slightly larger than the grapefruits, of a mottled red and sand color. It was cantaloupes, smeared with lipstick. This was disgusting, and worse were the bunches of table grapes in the next bin, for they too had lipstick on them. One could dig out the flesh of a cantaloupe and only soil one's hands or plate, but imagine trying to eat lipsticked grapes!

Thud, thud went the wilted heads of lettuce into the garbage. I suddenly realized—strange that I hadn't before—that I myself might be suspected of defiling the merchandise, especially if I were discovered examining it. But what sort of person would do such a thing? I wondered as I wheeled my cart away from the fresh produce into the canned goods. Passing the large cans of juice I came to the fruits. They can be convenient but I seldom buy them. I think I'm put off by the paper labels that often picture the fruit as larger than life-size and in colors that remind me of faded cloth. Then there were vegetables culminating in baked beans and then canned spaghettis and beefaronies, and then I came to the frozen foods.

These were in open-top freezer chests. As I understand it the chests can do without tops because the cold air inside, being heavier than the air in the room, stays in the chests the way water would. Whole turkeys and game hens in plastic skins were in one compartment. Their shapes made me think of a prehistoric stone carving I had once seen in a photograph, a fertility goddess I believe.

When I moved out at an angle into the space before the freezers I saw that on the white side of one of them the lipstick culprit had written "tsk tsk" in letters so tall and thin it was nearly illegible and beneath in thicker letters "pig," and there were some obscene words in smaller letters written with a paler more purplish lipstick. The very lipstick tube which had written the obscenities had been dropped on the linoleum tiles. The brand was good though the shade was no longer quite fashionable. I selected a frozen pizza. The other frozen packages shifted with a squeaky rustle and the freezer blew a cold breath up over my arms. It was time to go, I realized. I had a dentist appointment in the afternoon and before that I intended to do some gardening. Also Bob had wanted us to get in a little golf before dinner. What else was there I needed? Hamburger.

The meat was displayed along one side of the market in a bank of waist-high trays cooled from beneath. The trays are of noncorroding zinc perforated for drainage—there must be a gutter beneath. Around the row of trays is a rim of hard black rubber. Each tray is separated from its neighbor by a strip of not very clean plastic greenery. A passageway runs behind the meat counter, between it and the west wall of the market which unlike the other walls is of plywood and has mirrors set into it at regular intervals. Behind the wall are the meat lockers, mechanical sawers and slicers and other equipment for the store butchers. From the other side the mirrors serve as windows so the butchers can watch for shop-lifters.

First was the heart, tripe, gizzards and other cheap meats people in Verdant Park feed to their pets. Then came kidneys and liver and then chicken parts with their loose skin. The meats are packaged in styrofoam dishes covered with plastic wrap. Beyond the chicken were pink and grey chops with purple letters stamped into their borders of fat. Sometimes a little watery blood had leaked into a corner or stained the folds of trans-parent wrapping. Next came the vivacious red of steaks. The paper labels glued to the packages had three figures printed on them: price per pound, weight, and in the center the price of the piece of meat.

The hamburger is at the end of the meat counter near where a doorway leads back into the butcher shop. This door usually stands open so that the sound of grinding and thumping is more noticeable nearby, and also the smell of cold meat. However, the entrance corridor rounds a corner so that though I have sometimes leaned forward and squinted I have never been able to distinguish anything.

I selected a package of ground chuck and was turning to move away when the noise of a struggle caught my attention. Before I could move a group of angry people rounded a tier of shelves, brushing against it as they did and knocking to the floor several jars of a powdered substitute for cream for coffee, one of which shattered so that the white powder fanned out against the gray linoleum — and the three people bustled past me into the butcher shop so quickly that only after they had vanished did I have time to collect my thoughts and recognize what I had seen.

What I had seen was young Frank Smith, the son of my neighbors whose Irish setter I had watched earlier, being dragged along by two members of the supermarket staff, a heavy-set man and a woman. Ap-parently Frank was the lipstick writer — it was on his hands and face and on his clothing, and the employees seemed to have caught him in the act. Frank is a fairly attractive boy, an only child. He's in junior high now. There's too much age difference for him ever to have been a playmate of our children, and Bob and I aren't good friends of the Smiths' so that I know very little about the boy, but I certainly would never have supposed him capable of this sort of thing. I knew there had been some problems with his behavior in our Arbor St. elementary school, though never anything serious. While he seemed not to have many friends I knew he was a good athlete. Indeed here in the supermarket he had been wearing his grey flannel baseball uniform. The poor child had covered the crotch of it with a smear of the lipstick, had soiled his forehead and mouth with it and coated the palms of his hands. As the employees pulled him back into the butchery he had started to cry and to whine, "I didn't mean it."

From then until I drove into our driveway various questions were running through my mind. Why wasn't Frank at school? I remembered seeing his mother's car at the hairdresser. Perhaps Frank had stayed home because he hadn't felt well, and Marcy had brought him along with her to the shopping center. And yet, that being the case, it was surprising that she should have driven away, as I noticed she had done when I returned to my car. And where had the lipstick come from? Had he bought it? Had he stolen it from his mother or perhaps had she given it to him? And many questions of a quite different order entered my mind. I was in fact so preoccupied that I now can recall only fleeting impressions of the remainder of my shopping trip.

I remember the checker, a girl in her late twenties, still with a certain freshness about her face. Without a glance in my direction she said, "A shame about the kid with the lipstick." She didn't look at the cash register either, whose keyboard her right hand danced over brilliantly. Her eyes were searching out the prices on my groceries as she removed them with her left hand one by one from my cart, sorting them automatically as she did into the fragile, the frozen, the others.

Then I remember the grocery bags. Their color, the noises they made and above all their odor was like a relief, a wash of cleanliness and oblivion between me and the whole market and everything in it. Indeed at that moment the brown paper made me think of my parents, of their homely lives in their fragrant homely world, and made my heart yearn sickeningly backward toward them.

The drive home was full of dappling green sunlight. As soon as I arrived I telephoned Marcy Smith to let her know about Frank, but there was no answer. I was as much in the dark as ever — I might almost as well never have discovered who had done the lipstick markings. I unpacked my groceries, placing them in my cabinets, refrigerator and freezer. Then I sat down to drink a cup of coffee and rest and think.

Now if I may I'll tell one last story. It starts with things pretty much as they are. I was watering the lawn one afternoon and Bob drove home to tell me that a new president had been elected. He had pledged himself to reducing taxes, halting the population explosion, a soft landing on Venus and peace at any cost. Bob said, "We'll keep our fingers crossed."

It was peace that mainly interested us and so for the next year we tried to keep track of the various wars to see if they would let up any. A few seemed to but most dragged on without change or worsened, and some new ones sprang up. It was especially bad because one of the little wars in Africa somehow stirred up an epidemic of a certain fever that went right around the world. There were even some cases in America. Usually it wasn't fatal but its painful effects would persist for the rest of the patient's life. Finally though they did manage to develop a vaccine.

All the time things were growing worse. There was famine in east Africa and also in China—*Newsweek* had color pictures of people like skeletons kneeling to beg. We sent some money although we knew it wasn't even a drop in the bucket. Then in a short time—less than a month, really—it seemed limited war had broken out all over Asia. The paper carried a feature story, "Chinese Fight Like Animals," and showed an old man on all fours in marshy grass baring his teeth. That was in late summer. There were emergency sessions of the U.N. and conferences among heads of state. I took to carrying a transistor radio in my purse, paying attention to the news as I'd never done before.

The period was hard for parents. We did our best to insulate our children—guarding conversation, keeping newspapers in a locked cabinet —but inevitably they heard distorted rumors of what was happening. Even little Gavin came home from school and asked us about the Wu Han banquet. Priscilla must have been aware of more. Bob and I threw ourselves into arranging picnics and other diversions. The detergent rash on my hand spread because of my anxiety.

It was odd though. The situation suddenly worsened. Japan was drawn in, China split into two and then three states. A third of the population of Asia was gone and, fighting apart, disease and famine seemed certain to take another third. Clearly we were at a juncture of great historical importance and so we decided we owed it to the children to let them know about it. Still it was difficult for them but they seemed relieved that we no longer kept it all secret. They themselves saved part of their allowances to contribute to the Red Cross efforts.

Naturally everyone began to wonder whether we or any other major power would find it necessary to intercede. Japan, as I have said, was drawn in but other governments held back. China for years had seemed a threat to world peace and now the world seemed content to let China destroy itself. I knew little about the country beyond what I'd seen in movies and so I checked some books out of our Verdant Park public library and read up on it. The more I read the less I felt like reading, it seemed such a shame for so old and distinguished a culture to have fallen into such misfortune. Nevertheless I kept reading and learning and when Japan ceased to be autonomous I began to read about it too. The librarian and I grew to be friends of a sort.

At one point Bob's army reserve unit was mobilized and we felt sure we were going in, if only for pacification. Bob was even given shots for overseas travel but in the end nothing came of it and we resumed our routine of concerned watching.

There was the persistent worry that the Chinese might go beyond conventional warfare, but they never did. They quickly used up their supplies of ordinary weapons and still the fighting went on, dwindling but not ceasing until the beginning of winter when in one week hundreds of thousands died of exposure and illness. Then there must have seemed little left in the country worth killing for.

In southeast Asia and Indonesia, where the winter was less severe, the fighting continued. At China's demise the pro-Chinese forces in Indonesia, with no more ties to the mainland, sought simply to consolidate and establish themselves. But Australian commercial interests chose this moment to press for their complete eradication. What resulted was civil war in Indonesia. Simultaneously border war broke out between Cambodia and Viet Nam. Newspapers subsumed all these actions under the title of "the Asian civil war." Although, needless to say, it absorbed most of our attention, it was not the only war being prosecuted at that time.

There were periodic Arab-Israeli conflicts—the unfailing Israeli brio and Arab blundering tended to obscure for us the fact of the steady loss of life. Then there were two separate tribal wars in Africa, one a war of attrition and siege, the other a diffuse guerrilla action. Furthermore the long-expected revolutionary war in South Africa began. Here the world's first large-scale bacteriological warfare was carried out against the subject populations. Also there were pitiful bloodily suppressed attempts at revolution in Poland, Bolivia and Honduras. In Ireland, in the Caucasus and also Mongolia, along the French-Spanish border, and in the region around Montreal the frequency of religious and factional murder and riot was now so high as to be considered minor warfare by many commentators.

There was also war of a sort right here in America. In New York, Chicago, Los Angeles, and later Washington and Detroit there was first rioting and then almost continual fighting between the slum dwellers and the rest of the populace. Arson, looting and sniper shooting became common. In Detroit thirty-five starving black people immolated themselves together, in imitation of a similar act by seven hundred native Indians in Brazil. The poor in other U.S. cities demonstrated in sympathy.

There seemed to be a possibility of some national popular movement —revolution even—until the Christmas disaster in Chicago frightened people. For a week there had been clashes between the city's poor and the police and national guard. The poor had begun to employ a sort of guerrilla tactic—carloads cruising through better neighborhoods throwing incendiary bombs and doing other mischief on the run so that it was almost impossible to control them. Then toward midnight on Christmas Eve there came an explosion audible tens of miles away, lighting the sky over all Chicago, which destroyed several blocks in the center of the slum riot area and caused serious damage in a circle with a three-quarter mile radius. Two hundred people died instantly, a hundred more later and there were numerous injuries. Supposedly a shipment of high explosives had detonated by accident but the rioters believed the explosion had been planned as a punishment and warning to them. Most Americans believed such to be the case. Those who might have protested felt afraid so that even before the new year began the cities were quieter than they had been in months.

In January little Gavin had a viral pneumonia that worried us enough so that we couldn't attend news as closely as we might have wished. But I did save some newspapers and magazines, including one with the full text of the World Plea as it was called. The document had been drafted in Istanbul at the headquarters of the World Union, a rival U.N. which had sprung up. It was addressed to the people of the United States and called upon them to bend their nation's huge force in the interests of "us countless miserable dying ones." I found it very moving, the more so inasmuch as it was full of grammatical errors and strained un-American idiom.

Then I have an issue of *National Geographic* devoted to Asia. There were photographs of Chinese cities now entirely uninhabited. The views of snow falling on blackened ruins had an oriental quality. There was an article by a conservationist listing the species the war had rendered extinct. Hundreds and hundreds of square miles of previously arable land were now desert, of course. One scientist predicted that when summer came the change would affect weather around the world.

That issue had just been published when it became out of date as the eastern conflict flared up again. This time the action centered on Australia. British, Canadian, American, and Russian and various Asian troops and supplies were involved. It was summer there so that defoliation could be effective. The tempo of the bombing increased so quickly that dozens of newsmen, taken by surprise, died along with the combatants. By the end of January no one was left in Australia or New Zealand and it was estimated that these lands would be unfit for human habitation for half a century. The same was true of much of Indonesia and southeast China. However the engagement had been clean in the sense that nuclear weapons and, for the most part, biological ones had been avoided. Furthermore a quarter of the population including several aborigines was transplanted safely to Canada..

All this sounds terrible, and of course it was, especially since it seemed there was nothing we—Bob and I—could do. We had stopped sending money for relief, things looked so hopeless. In this connection I would say that Gavin's illness was a blessing in disguise because it was an enemy we could draw together against. One could write a whole story about the sacrifices Priscilla underwent, nursing and entertaining him. The neighbors were helpful too. Every few days Marcy Smith from next door would bring over something she had cooked for us.

China seemed to have suffered as much as possible already but toward the end of January war swept over it again. It was the first time the United States had taken unilateral action in the Asian civil war. Our president on live television explained that we would take "all necessary measures to protect China from foreign domination," i.e. from Russian troops and settlers massing in Siberia. Our bombs destroyed the ruins that stood as it were still warm from the earlier battles. There were few casualties because by then not many were left alive there anyway. The main effect was to render China like Australia and everything between uninhabitable for the forseeable future.

More serious was what happened at the edges of this battle. With increasing frequency bombers strayed into India and Pakistan and on occasion north into Siberia. There were exchanges of notes of protest and immediate Russian-American warfare seemed likely. Complex civil defense measures which I never quite understood were effected. Things looked especially grim when Russian troops carried out a fairly bloodless invasion of northern India. But suddenly everything seemed to shift. The catalyst must have been West Germany's and Italy's joint action against several eastern European communist satellites. Russia found herself over-extended and, I suppose, gambled on the chance that the United States would hold back unless attacked. Russian troops overran West Germany. Britain and France retaliated, launching American missiles with conventional warheads against the capitals of the communist satellites and then against Moscow and Leningrad. "World War III," said the paper's banner headline—though in reality the main fighting was only in Europe and Asia. Effectively we too were at war, though officially we were simply providing technical assistance. The month was known as terrible February almost before it had begun. Many army reserve units were called but Bob's happened not to be.

Moscow was the first city destroyed by nuclear bombing in this action. Berlin was next. The pope commanded all Catholics of whatever nationality to cease fighting but he died a few days later in the bombing of the Eternal City. I'd never been to Europe and when Paris was destroyed I sat up all night not knowing what to think, with tears running down my face. Soon bombs of every sort were falling all over Europe. I saw television coverage of when the Acropolis went. I remember pictures of crowds leaping into the Thames, trying to escape the fire storm from London. It was horrifying.

By the end of February matters stood roughly thus: except for Siberia, southern India and Sri Lanka, Eurasia like Australia had been depopulated and rendered uninhabitable. The same was true of most of northwestern

Africa and also of broad swaths across the south of that continent. There was scattered bombing and jungle fighting along the Amazon and a naval encounter off Chile. Eurasian nationals and some troops had migrated into Canada and Greenland and also, it was suspected, into South America. Africa was depopulated by the middle of March and India and Sri Lanka a week later. At the beginning of April North America was the only remaining significantly habitable land mass in the world. To ward off desperate invasion attempts we had widened the Panama Canal and left heavy artillery there and in the Aleutian Islands.

Now an unforseen difficulty arose. The bombs had almost all been delivered by planes or fired from ships and submarines — or, in parts of the battle of India, actually dragged into cities on huge wagons — so that our ICBMs remained intact. However their usefulness dwindled as the targets for which they were designed ceased to exist. Russia, we knew, and perhaps some other countries had emplacements of their own. We knew their general but by no means their exact location and for years the radiation would be too high for us to search them out. Of course we had missile defenses but the fact of those missiles waiting invulnerable in Asia and Europe made life in our cities, at which they were presumably aimed, the more nerve-wracking.

This tension must have been one cause for the renewed rioting that broke out. There was civil war in Mexico and most of central America, but Canada was comparatively quiet. Accordingly thousands of Americans from the east coast and from Chicago began heading there. The Canadian government put stricter limits on immigration and policed the border. Meanwhile dissatisfaction was overcoming fear of reprisals in U.S. cities so that, in spite of new incidents like the Chicago Christmas, civil disorder spread. States of emergency were declared in cities, counties, states and finally the entire country was under a sort of military rule. Since there had been no turmoil in Verdant Park we were spared the sight of troops in our streets.

The situation quickly worsened. The government found greater and greater harshness necessary. Public executions became common. Though much of the populace was passive, surprising numbers resisted as best they could. There was almost continual guerrilla radio broadcasting urging the people to take up arms and urging whatever forces there might be remaining in the outside world to attack America and liberate its people. All this was complicated by increasingly ruthless power struggles in our military-political regime with more assassinations and attempts at assassination than before.

Nevertheless in April things seemed to become calmer. The spring weather was beautiful. I would work in my flower beds and from moment to moment nearly forget what had happened. We scarcely dared hope or voice our hope. So ten or twelve days passed.

Then suddenly war came to America. Newsmen disagreed about the exact timetable but the rough order of events was as follows. Power stations, dams and industrial centers began to be destroyed with conventional but very large bombs. The government retaliated with "accidental" bombings, sometimes of entire towns. A rocket, probably with a nuclear warhead, came miraculously from somewhere in Asia. Our defense missiles intercepted it but soon after citizen sabotage irreparably damaged the radar system. Then it became impossible to defend against or even determine the point of origin of the missiles and, later, planes that began to attack our cities.

On television entertainment for the most part gave way to coverage of the war. Cities were evacuated but not quickly enough. I happened to be watching when the first nuclear weapon arrived. It was in Pittsburgh in the morning—I had just come back from driving the children to school. From the north out of a clear sky a tiny black dot increased in size and then fell below the horizon. Then there was the sonic boom and then I saw the brilliant fireball and almost immediately there came noise so loud I had to turn down the volume.

Rumors of all kinds spread. It seemed at least possible that some of the attacks were coming from Canada or Central America or Mexico, and so we launched missiles against those places. It was also suspected that our military in desperation had turned against the American people.

The wealthy and powerful retreated into their secret shelters. The government that remained was centered in the Rocky Mountains, as was the military. The ruined cities and countryside were ruled by roving crowds made savage and lawless by the radiation. Unchecked fires swept across thousands of square miles. The atmosphere was poisoned when government supplies of germ and chemical weapons were opened during the bombing of Denver. The president's plea for a truce was ignored and the fighting accelerated. I suppose the atrocities were no worse than those that had occurred elsewhere in the world but they seemed especially terrible for being perpetrated by and on Americans. There were no large cities left by late April.

Miraculously they didn't bomb Verdant Park or attack us in any way, though the rest of Kentucky suffered along with the nation. I had never traveled into those beautiful mountains in the east where Nadine grew up—Hazard, where she left her name in a bottle—and I had hoped they might be overlooked since they were so thinly populated, but there was no chance. I think the reason they spared Verdant Park must be this: if you look at a map of the United States you notice that it looks like an animal, with New England the head, Florida the forelegs and so forth. Now Kentucky stands for the heart and the state is even shaped somewhat like a heart. At the very heart of this heart is Verdant Park. I suppose if they left any part it seems understandable that it should be this.

In any case almost no one except for us was left by mid-May. The few who remained in shelters in the Rockies or elsewhere would soon die, whether or not they surfaced, from lack of food, the disease and poison in the air or the drifting radioactivity. The story ends with us in our living room in the evening—Bob and me and Priscilla and little Gavin gathered on the sofa before the television to look at the ruins.

IN THE
MIND'S EYE

WHEN SHE GRADUATED from high school Doris Fulkerson, valedictorian of her class and the only child of a prosperous widower, married Arnold Barron, who was somewhat below her. The Barron blood was reckless. Arnold's father had eked out a living with a little gas station but Arnold himself was ambitious. During World War I he took Doris off to Canada. He had a complicated scheme for making easy money from the war but luck was against him and after Doris became pregnant he caught pneumonia and died. Doris had barely enough cash and self-possession for the long journey home to Kentucky. When she arrived she discovered that her father too had died and that the war had ruined his business. As far as she knew she had no relatives anywhere, and certainly none in the town, which had turned against her on account of Arnold's wild venture. All that was left her was a small farm just outside the city limits. She sold half the land and then, living in the farmhouse, went into a seclusion to wait out her pregnancy and to think about what could be done with the rest of her life. She decided to take in laundry and to make use of her education by dealing in junk which she would call antiques.

When labor started she summoned a midwife and drank bourbon until she was unconscious. She awoke to discover she had given birth to twin boys. For ten dollars extra the midwife (who supposed that scandal was involved and the infants would be disposed of in some illegal fashion) agreed to maintain silence. Within the week Doris went to the courthouse to register the birth of a son, Victor, named after her father. This was in early June, 1918.

Carefully and in some desperation she had estimated the expenses of raising one child and she held to her plans regardless of facts as they were. She could have dispatched one of them with impunity but her solution was less direct, more imaginative and perhaps kinder. She simply recognized the existence of each on alternate days. Every other day each lived a normal life downstairs with her while upstairs his brother lay in the small rear bedroom ignored. She would interchange them in the early morning when they were still asleep and when she herself was as it were insufficiently conscious of what was happening.

Thus from the beginning, far prior to the reach of their memories, the twins were molded by an extraordinary pattern of life. One day each existed properly as a creature in his mother's attention only to return the following day to a suspended animation. They survived infancy because they were very hardy. Each of course was called Victor.

During what we may term the days of recognition each passed an agreeable time with Doris. Without regard to their age she discussed with them the most complex and adult matters as she cared for them or went about her housework, so that they commanded a large and sophisticated vocabulary. In her talks with them Doris returned most often to two subjects, their father and the community. From some necessity of her mind Arnold had become for her an ideal figure quite unlike the man she had married. She presented him to the twins as a fabulous inventor inspired with sacred genius; she made an apotheosis of his premature death. When she spoke of the community she emphasized its cruelty and its power.

School was the twins' first important contact with the world outside Doris's influence. They were suspicious and aggressive. Because neither had much use for other children it was some years before they began to perceive the peculiarities of their situation. They attended school, as they had done everything else, on alternate days. Since they were physically identical no one suspected that there were two Victors. Both were precocious but fairly early their interests began to develop in different directions, the one toward science, particularly mathematics, the other toward the humanities, particularly literature. It meant that "Victor," according to his teachers, was brilliant but erratic.

Doris had realized that, given the situation, words such as "yesterday" and "tomorrow" were bound to cause trouble, and therefore she avoided them. Thus in their childhood the twins were to an abnormal degree spared the idea of time. Such as they had, they would have developed primitively on their own with almost no help from the embodiment of the idea in the language. Matters were different at school. Inextricably mixed with all the other shocks of their first contact with the community were the teacher's magical outlandish words, "And tomorrow, children. . . ." It was easy enough to learn the names of the weekdays but the reason for the order in which they were taught was unclear to the twins, for whom the order naturally ran Sunday Tuesday Thursday Saturday etc. They asked no one for help with their problems, especially not Doris whom they loved and revered. But they began to feel that the world had huge mysteries in store for them.

Children are all conservative, and the twins were unusually so: through the first six years of their lives it occurred to neither to break with time-honored routine by seizing an opportunity—when Doris was out of the house—to climb the stairs and explore the little bedroom. But the confusion spawned by school made them adventurous and at last it happened. One winter afternoon Victor opened the door to find himself peeping sleepily out from a pile of blankets: Victor awoke from a nap to see himself standing in the open doorway. They stared at one another for several minutes. Then one closed his eyes and retreated beneath the blankets and one closed the door and ran downstairs.

It was so miraculous that for days they dared not hope for a repetition. One lay upstairs never turning his face toward the doorway; downstairs the other avoided the vicinity of the stair. But the strain was too great to last. This time instead of hiding or retreating they faced one another alike smiling a little doubtfully. They touched one another for reassurance. There was a corner of the back yard which, because it was in view of the back bedroom window, Doris had fenced off and forbidden them to enter. She had strung up a clothesline there, and it was where she stood, struggling to gather in a wash that had frozen. The twins watched her until she returned to the house, and then one of them slipped downstairs. They had not said anything but they had reached some understanding.

In the dead of the next morning when Doris rose to exchange the twins she found Victor's bed, beside her own, empty. Almost immediately Victor entered the room to say, "Don't worry. It's all right." Thenceforth the twins themselves carried out the ritual exchange. Doris must have been obscurely aware that they had discovered one another, had found her out. But there was an enormous compensation: she no longer needed by any of her reactions to recognize that there were two. Her madness had been accommodated. Her sons had taken it upon themselves and left her free for perfect consistency. From this time she seemed to take heart—the community remarked on it. There was a gala opening of her shop with a banner redundantly proclaiming "Mrs. Barron's Unique Antiques: No Two of Anything." It was something of a success. Not yet willing to befriend her, the local women nevertheless patronized her readily.

Now the twins spent much of their time together in the bedroom upstairs. They had a great deal to think over so that for some weeks they did not talk. It was a milestone when one said, "Miss Tackett asked me to recite the alphabet at school," and the other asked, "Did I do it right?" Once initiated, this form of communication (it was after all in a sense the logical one) prevailed. They never addressed one another in the second person, but always used the first, and always the singular. The peculiarity of their language manifested a genuine and deep peculiarity of thought. They simply did not conceive of themselves as distinct from one another in the way they were distinct from everyone else.

They knew Doris was not in their situation since there was no room in the house for any alter ego of hers. It did occur to them that other children might be like them. The evidence was against it—the fact that they alone had confused the order of the week—but for a long time they harbored the suspicion. Visiting their friends they would find excuses for exploring a home from top to bottom.

(Circumstances provided them with an innocuous introduction to the word "twin." There happened to be in the town a pair of nonidentical twins, a boy and a girl a few years older than "Victor." To Victor, then, twins were simply siblings who chanced to be the same age. It had nothing to do with their own case—indeed they did not think of themselves as separate enough to be siblings.)

"I didn't make any mistakes on the spelling test did I? What was the arithmetic assignment? Did I have fun at recess?" Doris had determined that the rear bedroom would be Victor's playroom and study; the twins spent their afternoons and evenings there talking, preparing their lessons from the same book. On rare occasions when a visiting schoolmate asked what was behind the door at the end of the hallway he was told that the room was an empty closet; the door was locked from the inside. As far as Doris was concerned the room may as well not have existed, for she no longer even came near the door. So with always greater caution the twins guarded the received status. "We played Red Rover—my team won. There's no arithmetic. I had a perfect spelling score—no one else did —Shirley missed 'cemetery.'"

Their secret would probably have been discovered if they had been engaged in a direct deception of the community, but they had no such simple intent. They did have a kind of secret but it was not the sort anyone was likely to suspect. It was not even something that could very easily be revealed. Already in their childhood the task of finding a way of publicizing the matter—finding words in the common tongue for it —would have been greater than the task of maintaining a vigilance to gloss over minor awkwardnesses. If something like duplicity was occasionally necessary, it was far more often the case that they told in good faith the only truth they could. "How does it happen that you do so much better than the other students, Victor?" asked one of their teachers. "I think," said Victor, "it's partly because my father was a genius, and then partly because I never think about just one thing at a time." The teacher repeated Victor's answer to friends as evidence of his originality.

The very idea of thought was difficult enough. The twins always believed that their minds were not completely separate, but it had become clear that they were in a sense divided. Both a cause and a consequence of this discovery was the fact that they grew less idle during the time they spent in the little bedroom. They thought about things; they read such books as they could find to interest them in the drafty run-down public library. And, having learned to talk to one another, they progressed naturally to the ability to talk to themselves. (There were thus for each some four grades of conversation: with the community, with Doris, with his alter ego and with himself, in order of increasing privacy. Grammatically, of course, the first two differed little and the last two were almost indistinguishable. Lexically their conversation with Doris differed from the other three: it was now only here that a vocabulary for dealing with time was absent. It may be this that made her endure in their minds, intense and fresh, even when they were adults.)

Their interests and abilities began to diverge as soon as they discovered that they had "sort of . . . two minds," at about age eleven in 1929 as the stock market crashed. One was drawn more to the exact sciences and the other to the humanities. The division was never absolute and as adults each remained *au courant* with the other's field. But once begun, the specialization was bound to increase if only because it was very profitable. "Victor," who had been an outstanding student, grew prodigious. For the next several years the slightly hushed tones in which her customers spoke of Victor made Doris herself whisper in her mind when she thought about her son. She stopped fondling him, she listened carefully to whatever he said.

When it came to fostering his talents she was at a loss. It remained to one of his teachers in secondary school (an ancient lady who taught him Caesar and Virgil and geometry) to take positive action. Largely as a result of her guidance Victor went off in the fall of thirty-six on the train to Boston and Cambridge, to the august Harvard College. Doris was prostrated with grief at his departure. The station-master said Victor himself seemed nervous: "He'd be sitting in the waiting room and the next thing I knew he'd be outside fidgeting around on the platform. And then when the train stopped he kept getting on and then getting back off, two or three times." The twins were in fact excited but they were not in the least frightened. As in separate cars they watched the changing terrain their thoughts were of their mother and of the triumphs of which they were by then fairly confident.

At first Harvard disappointed them. Perhaps they harbored some expectation of finding there at least others in their situation. In any case their disappointment was with the student body which seemed to differ not in kind but merely in degree from the schoolmates they had left behind. Still, the competition was sufficient to force a much greater specialization on them. The schedule of their alternation had to grow flexible—they might make the change several times a day.

Harvard itself during these years was in a transition. Victor Barron was one of the new breed that within a decade or two would dominate the college—the provincials, scholarship students of unknown families, drawn to New England out of nameless towns lost across the country, eager young men with nothing to recommend them but sheer learning and ability. Because almost everyone supposed Victor represented the thing coming for better or worse, they watched him with special interest. Despite the bustle of expansion and new building, Harvard in its flow of gossip and speculation was still much like the village the twins had left behind. It was soon clear to the community that Victor Barron was an article rather different from his fellow provincials. His success seemed effortless, nor was he apparently very ambitious. His form was eccentric rather than bad. Therefore he penetrated circles normally closed to his sort and so became familiar with the ways of the privileged. And when Victor was diffident in the face of social as well as academic success people concluded that he was not merely odd but also subtle and deep.

Meanwhile Doris became more ordinary. Expecting her to put on airs, people had hung back for a while after Victor's acceptance to Harvard was announced in the local newspaper. In fact, however, the clipping had come as the complete justification of her life, obviating further haughtiness. Victor had been launched and grieved, she had done her part; now she settled down to make peace and enjoy the rest of her life. Her replies to the profuse daily letters from her son grew perfunctory. When he wrote that he was doing research into the logic of relations, the philosophy of individualism, the figure of the doppelgänger, she returned her gracious approval though she had not an inkling of the meaning of his phrases. When acquaintances asked after him the information they received was agreeably vague—"No, no he doesn't have any particular young lady I don't imagine. I think he really has the bachelor's temperament—you know how these absent-minded scholars are." She was quiet, chatty and considerate. She renewed friendships of her schooldays. She thought of remarrying or taking a vacation.

The progress of the twins' specialization was as follows: one narrowed his interest in science to a concentration in mathematics, thence to the "foundations of mathematics," logic and set theory, and finally he settled in the difficult and then modish discipline of philosophy of mathematics. The direction of the other was a sort of mirro.-image—from the humanities in general to the study of literature, to aesthetic philosophy. Both in their final years at college proved able creators as well as scholars. In the fall of 1940 ominous with World War II there appeared in various Cambrige magazines and journals four works by V. Barron: an evaluation of Wittgenstein, a reevaluation of Aristotle's *Poetics*, a work of original mathematics entitled "Prediction in Unfolding Sequences of the Form 01101001 . . ." and "Mr. Hyde," a group of four witty and scandalous sonnets.

Doris's ease and her increasingly pleasant relations with the community produced a late bloom in her. Lines of strain vanished, she grew plump and even pretty. Therefore, and because the town had begun to realize that after the years of frugality she must have had a substantial sum tucked away, a number of prosperous middle-aged bachelors and widowers began to court her. It meant that with hints dropped here and there she was able to perform a considerable service for the twins entirely without their knowledge. They were puzzled by the announcement that Victor Barron had been deferred from the draft for reasons of health but they did not resent it. Unlike most of their contemporaries they were not eager to defend their country; furthermore romance at last loomed on the horizon.

The first year at Harvard had been monastic but the second saw the awakening of their interest in their Radcliffe classmates. They learned a great deal from a flirtation with Melissa and Felicia Machemer, identical twins from the Maine woods. In the back of Victor's mind was the timid hope that these shy pretty girls might have coped with a situation like his own. Communication in any case proved a greater problem than he expected. By this time, to be sure, the twins had seen the possibility of talking about and to one another with the system of pronouns they used for the rest of humankind. "It would ease my relations with the community in some ways," one said to the other, "but although they would think me suddenly more honest I should feel suddenly less so. The violence would be too great if I began speaking of myself as 'him and me' or to myself as 'you and I.' The words simply aren't honest or proper after all—they don't fit. Still, there will be difficulties with Felicia and Melissa." Difficulties there were, and the episode added to Victor's reputation for eccentricity, for Felicia and Melissa were voluble in their amazement. "At first we thought he was playing some joke. He practically hinted he had considered proposing to . . . *us both!*"

(One of the difficulties of telling their story is that much of what most aptly characterizes them seems trivial or even disagreeable—throughout their lives they felt most comfortable in the vicinity of mirrors. When as adults they thought back on their history the whole thing seemed to have an odor they remembered from youth: the chalk dust that lingered in empty classrooms through winter afternoons. It had the air of a childish and vacuous didacticism even when it set the teeth on edge. They sometimes seemed not like men but like thin girls.)

Upon arriving in Cambridge they had found rooms in a pleasant out-of-the-way narrow street; and since it had no longer been necessary for them to have two beds, they had one. In the beginning they slept together in the same spirit in which they had slept apart, but matters changed after Melissa's and Felicia's shocked failure to comprehend. They were well aware of the various categories of vice but had always maintained an effortless innocence, a sort of meditative distance. Now however one's hands wandered to the other as they lay side by side half awake. Still, they could not tell whether what they had discovered was vice or not: what they did together they would not have dreamed of doing alone or with another man. But they did not trouble themselves much with definition, and their passion followed its course unrestrained, accelerating until it absorbed them entirely and then subsiding to perfunctoriness and finally dwindling to almost nothing, all in the course of a month.

Such then was the background for their great love. Marie-Christine Dolanyi was one of those waifs of ambiguously aristocratic family who find their way to the Boston academy from all parts of the world. She had been born in Paris of generally Hungarian parents and had spent most of her life in London and New York. Her motley and exotic history augured well, the twins thought. Because she was thin and sallow and wore her hair long and pulled back, she had a certain questionable chic, but her features were not extraordinary; all this too seemed promising. Still the twins avoided rushing into explanations of their situation and they put off hints of anything so serious as marriage.

It went well. Marie-Christine was friendly and talkative; she and Victor enjoyed one another's company. She was a student of art history and aimed to be an architect, so that her interests nicely complemented those of both the twins. More important, her psychological and moral stance was as special as theirs though, as became evident, from different causes: where they sought that elusive set of consistent rules and standards adequate to their situation, Marie-Christine was discovering that she could cheerfully forgo any such quest, and enjoy not being able to predict what she might do from one moment to the next. The twins thought this the best omen of all.

In their letters to their mother they hesitated to mention Marie-Christine. Looking back on Doris through a considerable distance in time and space and experience, they had begun to reflect on her attitude toward them and to find it mysterious. A question they had never given much thought to now demanded attention: in what way exactly did their mother understand their position? It seemed eerily possible that she might view them in a way not very different from the rest of the world. They believed they could recall a time when she had supervised their daily interchange, and yet this might be an illusion. And yet—and yet there must have been a time, they reasoned, when she had supervised everything. But just this period was entirely beyond the reach of their memories. Their speculations gave them the odd feeling of having almost created themselves while at the same time paradoxically calling to their minds the bright shadowy figure of their father.

They sent Doris an experimental letter mentioning their interest in Marie-Christine. Doris's reply made no reference to the information. When at length they wrote more Doris replied, "I am interested to hear all your news." They wondered whether the increasing vagueness of her letters had been a strategic preparation for the moment at hand. They wondered, but they elected not to rush things with Doris any more than with Marie-Christine, and in their own letters they began to observe a careful silence regarding their romance.

In fact Doris's silence was partly studied. Her son's first mention of the girl had made her more uneasy than anything he had said before. At first she accused herself of a mother's selfishness. "After all," she told herself, "he does have to live his own life," and this consideration relieved her for a day or two. Yet when it came time to write Victor she found herself unable to speak of the matter. Perhaps it was her musing over the possibility of marrying again herself, or the fact that she had at last found a very secure and pleasant place for herself in the little community so that she could afford some unprecedented freedom in her own thoughts—for whatever reason, she began to wonder whether all was well with her son. "Maybe I've been unrealistic," she said to herself; "maybe I've idolized him too much." And she said to her close friend Hattie Partridge, "It's strange, he's my own son but I feel as if I don't know him. I can't help but think he'd wrong a wife somehow. Without meaning it, of course." Hattie couldn't conceal the fact that the statement seemed bizarre to her. Thereafter Doris kept her forebodings to herself, but they continued to trouble her. For a long time she had viewed her son much as the rest of the world did; but now as it were with a change in the weather the old self-inflicted injury to her sanity was acting up.

Marie-Christine moved into the apartment on Shepard Street in the fall of the twins' second year. It was to their advantage that she was absent-minded as well as chaotic and free and also that she had an incongruous sense of propriety: for the sake of appearance she kept an apartment of her own and gave a key to her lover. An old pattern asserted itself. Each of the twins slept one night in his own bed with Marie-Christine and the next alone in hers. She was everything they could have wanted, she was lazy and perfect. As early as ten they would trudge home from the library through the deep wet snow to find her asleep on the sofa before the fire.

A consequence of their liaison was that they saw less of one another than ever before. This mere physical separation affected them quite as strongly as their departure from Kentucky had done; but the effects were more subtle and gradual. Sometimes the separations lasted more than a week. In the climate of unorthodox speculation inaugurated by Doris's silence on the subject of Marie-Christine the twins began, only half voluntarily, to see their situation in new lights—a sort of aurora borealis seemed to play in both their minds. Especially during those minutes of the morning when they lay not yet fully awake beside Marie-Christine odd perspectives would open. For instance each might have the sensation that the other was little more than a figment of his imagination, a persistent dream.

And each began to consider the other's discipline from the standpoint of his own. The question they framed was, "What is to be done about. . . ." One completed it with "fiction" and the other with "logic." Whichever question was broached to Marie-Christine, she shrugged and said, "Why not worry about the real world." Their replies were much the same: "The real world takes care of itself." Marie-Christine said, "It's letting Hitler take care of it!"

The twins were in complete accord with her dismay; indeed they in their innocence were far more profoundly shocked than she who for most of her life had been intimately affected by vagaries of international politics. But for them the fact that the world was letting Hitler take care of it proved the irrelevance of personal action. There was nothing they could do. The problem, while presenting itself in terms of the practical, seemed immune to any attack in such terms—it seemed to lift itself by its own bootstraps into the realm of the theoretical. To them it was thereby more, not less, serious. And it was almost inevitable that they should see this problem in relation to the other that absorbed them. Thus there were times when each saw the other's chosen discipline as a force aiming at universal dictatorship, its demands granted through a policy of appeasement; and there were times when each saw his own discipline so.

Their concern for what might be called the international politics of the mind partly bridged the new distance between them occasioned by the mechanics of living with Marie-Christine. As though for a series of diplomatic talks they began to seek one another out; their talks were successful because they spoke in good faith unlike real diplomats. It turned out that something more exciting than peaceful coexistence was possible and even, as they thought, necessary. What was indicated was for the disciplines to renew themselves by subsuming one another, since their aims finally converged. Literature and philosophy were to become more like one another, especially in their format: investigating philosophical problems was to involve constructing fictions and vice versa. In all this the twins were children of their time more than they knew.

Their rapprochement began in the winter and lasted into spring with every promise of continuing indefinitely. Marie-Christine suspected Victor of philandering: the occasional untruthfulness with which they glossed over the time they spent together failed with her. And yet she was not jealous—in fact she was pleased to think of her young man's gaining a bit of what seemed to her salutary experience. And she had nothing to complain of since his attentions to her were if anything increased. She was beginning to realize that Victor was very satisfactory indeed and she was considering the possibilities of a long-term association with him. Thus all three of them felt pleasantly on the verge of something as the Cambridge weather made its fitful and lovely progress toward summer.

In May, excited and fortified by these developments, the twins renewed their attempt to elicit from Doris some formal recognition of Marie-Christine. Since strong measures seemed needed they went a little beyond the facts and spoke of a probable engagement. After a week's silence came a reply. The twins read it together.

"I expect you have wondered that I've not said anything about your young lady before this. Well, it was partly that I didn't quite know what to say. Then too I felt it would be wiser to wait a bit in case she was merely the sort of passing fancy young men seem so prone to nowadays. (I've tried to think what your father would have done.) I see now that your interest in her is not at all frivolous.

"I should also say, Victor, that I have been a touch uneasy to think of your marrying—but we'll talk about that when I see you—you're just so unique I have a hard time trying to imagine what sort of wife would be right for you—I hope you'll write and tell me more about Marie-Christine—but we'll talk. In fact we've a great deal to talk about.

"I had hoped to come to Cambridge for your graduation and to meet Marie but I'm afraid it won't be possible. I haven't been as well as I should be—don't alarm yourself, I haven't mentioned it because it's nothing very serious—but Dr. Finley says I ought not make the trip. Maybe it's for the best, as I'm not sure I'd know how to behave among all those people up there. Still, it's a great disappointment. I'll be glad to send a letter of explanation if there's any sort of ceremony that requires my attendance.

"But I have thought of a plan to make up for this. I suppose you intend to come home to visit for some part of the summer. And so I would like you to invite Marie to come with you, so that we can get to know one another. She could stay in the back bedroom, or I could arrange other lodgings for her—whatever is convenient. I don't know just how much rail tickets cost now, but I've enclosed a check that ought to cover your fare at least. I want this trip to be my graduation present to you.

"I know this place won't seem very exciting to a young lady familiar with the capitals of Europe—but if you can convince her to come, I'll do what I can to divert her."

One of the twins said, "It's reassuring . . ." and the other continued ". . . but somehow not so much as I'd expected." Doris's check was generous—the total something above the price of three round-trip tickets.

Marie-Christine had planned to spend the summer with friends on Long Island but she was easily persuaded to come to Kentucky which seemed as exotic to her as Europe seemed to Victor. Further, an instinct told her that meeting Mrs. Barron would reveal much about Victor. The twins by this time were such virtuosos at juggling themselves on trains that Marie-Christine's presence simply added zest to the performance. Yet as the train pulled out of South Station they looked out on Boston with a nervous melancholy. More than ever before in making this trip they seemed to be leaving a world of brisk airy freedom and returning to a region fenced with the dumb rigors of the heart. There might not after all be room for Marie-Christine, they thought.

The house had been refurbished top to bottom—fresh paint, modish new drapes, and everywhere the "antiques"—ink bottles on the mantlepiece, trivets and serving trays and other kitchenware on the walls, a bouquet of gramophone speakers in a corner and a genuine cow-catcher on the hearth. Doris seemed timid but ceremonious and efficient. By a stroke of luck her neighbor Frieda Kirkwood was away for the summer, leaving her house vacant. Marie-Christine could stay there. Victor could return to his old room, and use the back bedroom for a study—there was still a bed there if he wanted a nap. The old Dodge had been repaired so that the young people could visit scenic spots in the area.

The first days passed in a clutter of arrangements and obligatory social calls. Doris bided her time and attempted no more than the most polite small talk with Marie-Christine; but she watched with interest. Though the community was awed by the girl's accent and her foreign manners, when she turned out to be "not on her high horse one bit" but friendly and rather open, they were charmed. Doris too was beginning to be charmed. "Whatever she does she looks as if she's in a picture," Doris said to Victor, and there was a wistful fall in her voice.

One of the twins was always at the Kirkwood house reading, writing or daydreaming. In the evenings he would slip out to wait in the dark for an hour and then reenter pretending he had crept away from his own

100

house. They alternated regularly. The time spent alone was especially thankful as a relief from contact with the townspeople. The twins were not entirely pleased with Doris's new sociability—her reconciliation with the community seemed to compromise her a little in their eyes. And they would have preferred it if people had taken to Marie-Christine less readily.

As things quieted, Doris and Marie-Christine sought occasions to be alone together. At first the twins encouraged this both because they were curious to see how the women would react to each other given a chance for greater intimacy and because it enabled them (the twins) to be together.

Doris was thirty-eight and she had decorated herself, manner and body, with gewgaws somewhat like those cluttering her house. Marie-Christine in the full flower of her youth was easy-going to the point of being streamlined. They sat in the kitchen and sipped coffee. By fits and starts Doris tried to sound out Marie-Christine on the subject of Victor. The girl was friendly but, it seemed to Doris, noncommittal. Doris fished with "I think you must be the first young lady he's taken a genuine interest in." Marie-Christine chuckled. Doris raised her eyebrows and watered her African violets.

"He was very much out of the ordinary here, as you might imagine. I suppose some people found him . . . peculiar, or . . ." Doris said. Marie-Christine nodded and said, "I think some people in Cambridge found him peculiar also. May I ask, does this surprise you?" "Not exactly. . . ." In a moment Doris said, "Won't you have some more coffee, Marie, and listen to a word of wisdom, such as it is, or advice. You young people appear to have become fairly well . . . infatuated, haven't you? What I would suggest (I hope you take this in the spirit in which it's meant) is that it would be well for you to . . . scrutinize one another a little more carefully. Young people who are admirable in themselves don't always have altogether the best effect on one another; in spite of their good intentions. I suspect there's a great deal you don't know about Victor—a great deal no one knows. . . ." "You sound almost ominous!" "Yes, I do," said Doris.

Marie-Christine's curiosity was aroused. She described the conversation to Victor. "What do you suppose?" she said, "—that it's really me she's worried about, and not you? We *have* 'scrutinized' each other more than she knows, haven't we? You know, I do like her—far more than I'd expected to, and I can't help but be troubled by this mysterious anxiety of hers. Victor, let's stay here for the summer—I feel as though she might need some help we could give her."

I have related the foregoing as if I were some sort of semidetached observer, partly because it seemed that only through such a fiction could I set forth the events described so that they would be comprehensible to the ordinary reader. However I think by now the fiction (wearisome to me from the beginning) has served its purpose and can safely be abandoned, so that I shall henceforth speak in my own voice and from my own viewpoint. I hope the relief I feel won't lead me into unnecessary expansiveness. But I do want to try to be faithful to things as they happened. I wrote the preceding section in bits and scraps during July. It is now the second week in September, and since I have no immediate plans I should be able to finish the story in a day or two. I am still rather in a daze and this writing may help dissipate some of the shock and clear my mind.

What stands out most in my memory of these past weeks like an emblem for everything else that happened is Marie-Christine's face which seemed to grow lovelier as it showed more strain, bewilderment and fatigue—as though she were a flower whose delicacy was manifest only in its wilting. While the sun browned Mother and me it seemed to bleach her skin—by the first of September she was paler than I had ever seen her—the very blue of her eyes looked lighter.

The whole thing seems to shift and fall apart and regroup in my mind as I think back on it—we all somewhat lost our self-possession, we all grew somewhat feverish and harried and now I feel weak and drained but relieved. The paper predicts a week's rain—it is raining now, a slow chilly rain. I have lighted a fire—I feel weak, but since I am both ambidextrous I can shift the writing among four hands. I shall clear my mind and begin while the fire burns and the rain falls. I shall finish the tale. Perhaps it is hardly necessary: perhaps the conclusion was foredestined and is apparent to the discerning eye—in general, at least—the peculiar alloy of triumph and failure. But the particulars are of interest and I shall finish the tale.

Boston now seemed a sweet romance. The future had began to rush and to demand decisions to fill its vacancy. I felt my age—I felt it was time for me to reap some comfort and security after my long adventure. I did not want to have much to do with the "real world" but I did want a certain minimum ideally embodied, I thought, in Marie-Christine. I would certainly have wished to give Mother any help I could, "but not," as I told myself, "at the expense of my entire happiness." Still I could not very gracefully bustle Marie-Christine off and so I agreed to stay. If the summer proved an ordeal I would meet it with the assurance that it would be the crucial one. And I was curious. "What will happen? How might I react? I can't say, but there's this: it's hardly conceivable that I won't discover something of importance—that I won't somehow solidify."

Marie-Christine did her best to reassure Mother by explaining that we were cognizant of the perils of young marriage but that after all we were not young by local standards and we knew one another very well indeed. The next day I managed to be alone with Mother—it was difficult—and I took much the same line. Also I told her I found it strange that she should have spoken to Marie-Christine the way she had. "It seemed to me you almost gave her a warning—why did you do that, Mother?" It was the closest I had ever come in my life to discussing my situation with her. She shrank into her chair and avoided looking at me for several awkward moments and then said, "I'm not sure, Victor. It's only that she's such a nice girl. . . ." Then she flushed violently, staring at me with wide appealing eyes.

It was clear that she was telling the truth—she *wasn't* sure. At last I was certain that for some twenty years she had been not merely subtle but also self-deluded—had looked away from the truth with the firmness of insanity. Of course this enormously saddened me for it proved that I was alone after all—I had been taking sustenance all that time from a purely imaginary sympathy and understanding. But what intrigued and even alarmed me was the fact that Mother's rigid madness seemed to be breaking up—she didn't yet know the truth but she had felt its pressure. My understanding of these things gave me a tactical advantage of sorts.

Marie-Christine's state of mind was less clear to me. Of course she must have been in a general way aware that I was far from conventional. I sometimes toyed with the possibility that she might have an instinctive comprehension of the exact nature of my situation. I supposed it would be a shock forced suddenly on her consciousness but I imagined her quite capable of absorbing such a shock. Nevertheless I thought that if the revelation must come it would be better when she and I were on our own away from the tensions of my home. Therefore my first thought was to smooth Mother's ruffled spirit. For a few days my placid demeanor, my solicitous attentions seemed successful, but soon her eyes told me this was insufficient.

After some thought I hit on a strategy of diversion. The general idea came to me in a flash—I was rehearsing to myself a conversation between Mother and Marie-Christine which I had overheard. They had been chatting about Marie-Christine's relatives, and she had described an uncle who, having demonstrated great flair for business, had disappointed the family by dying young. What now struck me was that the talk had then continued to meander: Mother had not seized the opportunity to lament the similar case of my father. As I thought about it I realized that scarcely a word had been said about him since we had been home. Furthermore, when I skimmed through the huge packet of letters Mother had written in the past four years I saw that after the first year there had been a decline in such observations as "your father would be proud," a decline so gradual that I had not even remarked the fourth year's lack of any mention of him. Poor mother! I seized and played on this point of apparent weakness a little ruthlessly.

The next evening at dinner I turned the conversation once more to Marie-Christine's uncle. Mother said, "It must have been a terrible misfortune. I always have such sympathy for . . ." and then she stopped, staring at us wonderingly and foolishly in the candlelight. ". . . for such misfortunes," she went on. Marie-Christine said, "Do you feel unwell, Mrs. Barron?" "No, my dear."

I nourished the seed I had planted with scattered sentences—"Didn't this belong to my father?"—spacing them widely in the hope that I might play the thing out over the entire summer. Mother's reactions were marvelously various. Sometimes she snatched eagerly at the opening and tried to lead me into talk of my father; but then I would grow distant and uninterested. Sometimes she virtually flinched and then I would press her a bit more. Marie-Christine said, "I think I see what you're up to, but are you sure it's the best way to help her? Aren't you upsetting her needlessly?" I said, "Anything worthwhile is bound to be painful."

Indeed the treatment proved more tonic than I expected or wished. One afternoon while Marie-Christine was napping I had been helping Mother with her gardening. We were resting on a little wrought-iron bench surrounded and partly shaded by the bean poles. Before I saw what was happening—before I could prevent it—Mother began to call my bluff. She was fanning herself, and out of the blue she said, "There's something, you know, that's been on my mind, and I've thought we ought to speak about it—in strictest honesty, Victor, that your father would have been—was—really a genius, strictly speaking, you know, *can't* be proved—since he never had a chance to prove it himself. Of course I had faith in him, but then a proper wife always does, and I think now that in the early years of my grief" (she actually used these words) "I may have exaggerated his promise. It's something I've realized clearly only in the last few days, Victor—I believe you've suspected something of the sort yourself, haven't you?—anyway I feel better now that we've straightened it out. I imagine you'll want to talk it over with Marie."

This surprised and shocked me—I certainly hadn't suspected it. I had tried to guess the reason for her uneasiness about my father, but this sort of thing had never entered my mind. Instinctively I thought, "She's lying," but I saw that she was not. She had been speaking rapidly and breezily, staring into space, but now that she looked at me I saw that if anything she had been softening and glossing over the whole truth. I could think of nothing to say—I could hardly think at all. For a moment I simply sat and watched her. She had dropped her fan. Among the soft heart-shaped bean leaves, lacy with worm holes, she seemed like something in a mad dream—a middle-aged princess staring out of a flurry of grey green valentines. I hurried away to the Kirkwood house where I could be alone with myself.

When I had recovered my self-possession I decided that it behooved me to play my shock for all it was worth. It seemed bizarrely possible that what had been troubling Mother was just the necessity of making this revelation about my father—in any case I had to try to make her believe so. I thought it would be well to make Marie-Christine think so too. I did not need to dissimulate my own turmoil—I merely showed it. I returned home preserving a quiet dangerous demeanor. Mother and Marie-Christine had conferred and they eyed me anxiously. Meanwhile back at the Kirkwood house I was beginning the first sections of this story. That night Marie-Christine comforted me—"You oughtn't take it so hard, and think of her—she's at her wit's end—she had no idea." I promised to do what I could. I was genuinely very depressed though. I must have payed little attention to anything but memories of my child-hood, for now I find myself unable to recall much of the days immediately following Mother's revelation. I think she kept largely to her shop and I know Marie-Christine did what she could to ease things for everyone.

A mathematician named Gödel had recently done a rather spectacular proof of a new theorem. Roughly what this theorem said was that any logical system generates comprehensible statements which can neither be proved nor disproved within that system. I felt as though my life had meandered into this sort of unevaluatable statement. When I considered the literature I knew the closest thing to my state of mind and emotion seemed to be George Eliot's Baldassare in whose anguish and senility the very meaning of language would flicker and vanish. Like that old man I needed revenge, it seemed. But even this idea was a disturbance always at the edge of my vision, impossible to focus.

It's more and more difficult to continue. Something of the feelings I had then keeps coming back to me—the feeling that it was all alike from beginning to end so that I don't need to know any more. I remember we were all extraordinarily quiet—in fact toward the end we hardly said anything—and yet then, and now, it felt like being in the center of a noisy argument, being caught in crossfire of loud senseless assertion, knowing it was going to keep going on without any agreement's being reached. And yet we grew quiet as mice toward the end.

The feeling of noise grew especially intense at times like that when I came upon Mother braiding Marie-Christine's lovely hair in the grape arbor. It made me feel I had a hangover. Something had to be done. I returned to the Kirkwood house and talked it over. Something had to be done, otherwise it seemed Mother's madness might leave her to possess me. I felt like saying to Marie-Christine, "Hitler indeed! How can I think about him at a time like this?" Clearly we would have to leave, she and I, for our sakes, regardless of what it did to Mother. And I had begun to fear that Mother's illness, her physical illness, whatever it was, was bogus. I hardly knew what to do other than leave. I found Marie-Christine and made love to her and told her my plans.

"Perhaps you're right after all," she said. "I don't like to say it, but when she was handling my hair I felt uneasy. I didn't enjoy having her touch me, I don't know why. But I won't have a scene, darling, not with her. I mean to say I'd sneak away some night rather than that."

At dinner she looked lovely and very happy. Mother said, "I hope Victor found some way to entertain you this afternoon my dear. You must be finding it tedious here. . . ." For a moment it looked like an opening but then it began to look more like a lure or even a dare although Mother did look more sad than defiant. But I had started to talk and couldn't very well stop so that somehow these words came out: "You know, there must be comedies that are ugly through and through."

A few days passed. Mother seemed to be waiting. At last I said something like "Marie-Christine has to return to New York next week, and. . . ."

"You've been a charming guest, my dear, and we shall certainly be sorry to see you go," etc. I let it pass for the moment but the next day I told Mother I planned to go east for a while too. Timidly she said, "I don't think you ought to, Victor. I've been thinking, you know. . . ."

"Dear mother," I said, and embraced her—she cowered like a kitten or a puppy in my arms—"You mustn't worry yourself about my plans. I've always appreciated your thoughtfulness but you know I have to plan for myself now."

"Stay, Victor," she pleaded. "I'm worried. There's so much we should discuss. Things will work out, I'm sure they will." Unfortunately Marie-Christine entered in time to hear and misinterpret the last sentence. She said, "Oh, Victor, you've told her. I was afraid you wouldn't approve, Mrs. Barron. But this is lovely. You must start planning to come to New York for the wedding. I hardly have a family to speak of but my cousins are there."

"I don't think I could travel so far," Mother said and then she fainted.

"Poor dear," said Marie-Christine. "Well, then, we can have the wedding here I suppose." I felt like explaining nothing. We put Mother to bed. I left Marie-Christine to revive her and I went to the Kirkwood house to think.

Only now does it occur to me to wonder what Mother said to Marie-Christine when she revived—at the time it hardly seemed to matter. I simply had to give up control, rest for a while, let happen what would. I believe it was toward evening, and raining. I think it was then I marked a quotation in a book I was reading, to be included in this story:

*Die tollsten Fieberphantasien, die kühnsten Erfindungen der
Sage und der Dichter, welche Thiere reden, Gestirne stille
stehen lassen, aus Steinen Menschen und aus Menschen
Bäume machen, und lehren, wie man sich am eignen Schopfe
aus dem Sumpfe zieht, sie sind doch, sofern sie anschau-
lich bleiben, an die Axiome der Geometrie gebunden.*

Then there were some days in which everyone felt gloomy and disgruntled and kept largely to himself, and when any of us spoke it was
abruptly, out of the blue:

Marie-Christine: "Make her see I'm not as she supposes. Who does she
think she is to tell me about wickedness?"

Mother: "I must forbid your marrying, her, Victor, there's nothing else
I can do. Victor, I have been a madwoman—how did you let me become
so confused?"

Me to Mother: "I love and pity you and honor you but you have given
up your right. We'll leave soon and you must reconcile yourself."

Marie-Christine: "I won't be alone with her, Victor."

Marie-Christine: "We must manage it without a scene, for my sake. I'm
such a coward."

Me to Marie-Christine: "We can just get on a train and vanish. We're
young."

The time seems broken with such remarks. Sometimes some of us
mumbled so that we could scarcely be heard. When I was alone I called
myself "we" for the first time. It proved easy and meaningless. I felt like
something which is meant to shed light and does not.

There were ironies I scarcely noticed then but which please me more
now that I think about them. Mother, taking drastic action to prevent the
marriage she thought wrong, sought support from her friends among the
townspeople. I heard about it from Roy Struthers who with much hesita-
tion told me he thought she needed "looking after" since she seemed to be
"wandering." "Poor thing, she was insisting you had a twin brother and
that I had to keep you from going off with that nice girl to get married. I
humored her, I thought that would be best."

And so she herself provided the suggestion for what finally gave me a
kind of trump card. She had grown absolutely determined. She even
admitted what she had been up to: "I've talked to some people already,
told them you shouldn't get married. You know it's because I love you
Victor, and it's tearing me apart but I know what I must do. If you leave I
will follow you, I'll tell everyone on the train, I'll tell people in New York,
I'll write to Harvard College, I owe it to you both, and to myself. . . ." She
burst into tears. Marie-Christine said, "Ah Victor, but I can't have this.

You must work it out with her. I'll leave in a few days and then if you can work it out you come too." Of course she was a terrible coward but it made me only love her the more. And so the next day I arranged to have Mother committed to a "rest home" in a town nearby. How she shrieked when they came for her! Roy Struthers did his best to quiet her. It was early in the morning—we thought it would be easier if she were drowsy. It was in fact the hour when I used to come creeping down or up the stairs. But the noise awakened Marie-Christine and she insisted on finding out what was happening. "It's the best thing," I explained. "You can see she'd have brought it on herself eventually. She'll be well taken care of."

"I see," said Marie-Christine, very gravely. A few days later she was gone. I should never have let her out of my sight I suppose but things seemed to have worked themselves out and I was exhausted. She said I had gone "really too far," and that she had to leave, I would not be able to locate her, perhaps the love would come back and she would write, perhaps not.

Furious and disgusted, I had Mother brought back home but we could not bring ourselves to say much to one another. I suppose she had little energy left anyway. She proved to have been in bad health after all and she died not long after. This is another of those odd ironies: things really were working out unbeknownst to Marie-Christine and me. I suppose Mother felt she was dying and for that reason was especially frantic toward the end.

Now I want to quarrel a little with a certain sort of reader of my story. I know the world is full of people like Marie-Christine, inclined to make the sort of objections that rouse me to replies like, "How can you expect me to worry about Hitler at a time like this!" I mean that there are people who will suppose my story to be folly of the worst kind. I want to anticipate their objections by saying, "Folly's not so easy to pinpoint as all that, would that it were." I maintain that it's no good merely to explain things away because they can always sneak back. We ought to work through whatever comes to hand in good faith and not go flying off after something else just because nobody would call *that* folly.

First I ought to say that I've begun to suspect that the real problems and issues may be quite different from what I had supposed. Looking at things from this end alters the perspective. When interesting men play billiards one watches the table of course whether the play is good or bad or simple or intricate, and yet all the time it's only the game in the men's minds that's of any importance. So with Marie-Christine and me, except that even our emotions and opinions were like the billiard balls at play, and the important game is the retrospective one in my mind now. Surely the events matter less than what I think about them.

In a way the real question was whether things would be disastrous. If the story has a primary moral I think it must be this: avert catastrophe. Hold back, maintain the dispassionate eye when your life seems to lean out. In the Alps Antony for all his custom of luxury ate "strange flesh, which some did die to look on." We know so little that there is no point in drama and in particular none in catastrophe. The only final solution is an empty one like Hitler's suicide.

I can't say whether I'll see Marie-Christine again. I'm of a mind to remain here for some time and it would certainly be convenient if she came back. When people ask after her I give them elaborate, varying and contradictory lies to explain her absence. It's been a painful process but I've finally learned that there is almost no limit to almost everyone's credulity. The other evening I went out for a walk together. Old Elias Leeper my neighbor saw me and promptly sat down on the sidewalk and began shaking his head and pounding on it with his fist. An automobile caught me in its headlights and careened wildly. I returned home, for the townspeople's safety.

Marie-Christine and I could live here comfortably whether or not I confronted her with the full truth of my situation. In fact I could see us settling down here in pastoral retreat, enjoying our subtleties, watching them grow outdated—perhaps we'd raise interesting children. Part of the point I want to make is that I'm unwilling to predict anything more than that things will continue for me in one intriguing form or another and that I shall continue to try to deal with them.

Another of the real issues of my story seems now to have been that of language. I write these words in a period which is seeing parallel movements in literature and philosophy—in both realms attention is turning toward *ordinary* language. These movements are being hailed as revolutionary, and doubtless they are. In any case my history has been that of an extraordinary being confined to ordinary language. It has enabled, even forced me to maintain the illusion that I am like other people. But this means that ordinary language has failed everyone else with respect to me—or has it? What shall I say here? The question is surely of the trustworthiness of ordinary language.

One further point also has to do with ordinariness. As I look back over what I have written I notice that in a way this has been the story of my peculiarity. But what I have known all along, and what I've finally learned to codify for myself, is that the ways I differ from other people are much less important—even much less noticeable—than the ways I'm like them. And I have made a resolution, which may be the major consequence of all the events I've described: I intend to *be more like other people* as much as possible, and this will surely be the great undertaking of my remaining life.

109

BRIGHT GLANCES

I WAS BORN Margaret Rideout in Earlington, Kentucky, in 1933.
My father worked conductor for the L&N Railroad that came through
Earlington then and even stopped for cargo and passengers. My mother
clerked drygoods downtown at the company store when I and my
younger brother Eddy were growing up. When I was fifteen I swam
across black cold deep Earlington Lake. There was a beach on the town
side then and over along the railroad crews kept the bank cleared.
Today the whole lake must be full of snakes. I had on my black lisle
bathing suit and white rubber cap with a chin strap and raised roses at
the temples. Two of my girlfriends witnessed it. Years later someone
meeting me would say, "Hey wait a minute: were you the Margaret
Rideout that swam Earlington Lake?" My girlfriends cheered across the
water when I climbed up under the trestles. I should swim back, they
shouted. I just waved and followed the hot tracks down to where they
crossed the road and then followed the road back up into Earlington.

Poppa died around that time. Eddy had run away so there was only
mother and me left but the house seemed smaller if anything. I missed
both our men. Eddy was small for his age and private. His note said love
and said when he was rich he'd buy us all Buicks. We had fished together
after school through the war—never caught much more than sunfish out
of Earlington Lake. I missed Eddy and told myself stories about where he
was and what he was up to.

I missed Poppa too though not so much since he'd usually been on the
trains anyway. He had a heart failure out of Nashville and came home

the next day in the refrigerator car. The cemetery took him like it owned him. I remember thinking the train must have been whistling into a tunnel and Poppa must have spread his wings and risen straight up over the mountain with his eyes toward Earlington. I grieved Poppa but more I simply missed him. I missed the whole family going out to the Indiana Tavern on the road to Evansville twice a year and having Lucille Salmon there call us all by name. It was a long drive, twenty miles maybe. We had a big old Pontiac, and then another. In the back seat Eddy'd look out his window and I out mine, like dogs, and I'd think what a wonderful surprise we were about to give Lucille Salmon. They had a woman playing requests on a Hammond organ. We ate fried chicken and french fries. But always when we walked in the door I felt proud and shy when Lucille Salmon exclaimed, "Well Lawrence! Well Edna! And look how Maggie and Eddy have grown!"

I remember one time Mother was at prayer meeting and I went into the parlor and looked at a book Poppa had used to read when he was home and Mother was reading the Bible. It had a green cloth cover, and was called *One Thousand Beautiful Things*. The things were stories and pieces of stories, and poems about flowers. Poppa probably hadn't read the poems because he never cared much for flowers. We sent a postcard about Poppa's death to Eddy's last address, but it came back.

The week after the burial Mother and I went to hear the will at Utley and Hickman law office down on Railroad Street up over the barber shop. I'd never set foot there before. Books made Orrin Utley's office smell funny, but otherwise it could have been any office. The window looked out on the L&N water tower. Mother got everything of course. Mr. Utley looked like a preacher with his black hair and black eyebrows and blue chin. At first I thought the blue was light reflecting up from his three-piece suit.

How old must I have been? 1949—sixteen, I'd done creditably in Caesar and knew some algebra and plane geometry. Orrin Utley asked me to his Wednesday night Carmelite prayer meeting the next week. The church was cold and noisy. Orrin walked me home under the elms that lined the street then. On the sidewalk in front of our old cast-iron yard fence he said Maggie, lawyering's lonesome even if I do know more than I'd like of my clients' lives. You Maggie could help a shyster (he wasn't one) to probity, and married you'd flourish more than under your mother's tutelage. Come live with me in my house on Hall Street, Maggie.

I said yes. I'd seen what Mother and Poppa and other couples in that coal-dusty little town let show about marriage, and I'd guessed some of the rest.

We went to Seebree, where Orrin's sister had an empty house, for the honeymoon that lasted two days till Orrin had to be back at his office for a deposition. That Seebree house, at first I thought we were going to live there and I was anxious and relieved at the same time. No elms, no other house in sight, the road gravel and dirt. It was in a field, and had canned soups on a shelf over the kitchen window that looked out over the tobacco fields into the hardwood woods under a cold sky. I looked out into that permeable wall across the ploughed field, and I wondered what in the world I'd gotten myself in for. Fall starlings were rooting in the field. I remember the house didn't yet have electricity. In the upstairs bedroom Orrin was dimming the kerosene lamp and I was turning back the bed and he said Maggie, you know what a man and his wife are supposed to do in bed?

In fact older Earlington girls had given me hints behind the brick schoolhouse. Orrin's back was white, and his feet but elsewhere mostly he was black-haired as could be. Seebree Kentucky, I remember thinking, you took my maidenhead. Undress, Maggie, Orrin said, and then he didn't want me to put on my nightie. It went the way most wedding nights must. Once by accident he caught me under the chin with his shoulder so I bit my tongue and tasted my warm weak blood. Rending the veil hurt, but there was enough love in that attic room for me not to care. When we put on our nightclothes and fell asleep, Orrin had his arm around me.

So I didn't finish my high school but settled down to being a lawyer's wife and keeping house. All the same they invited Orrin and me to the senior prom. It was funny to hear my old classmates call him Mr. Utley. My formal was strapless pink tulle shading to a deeper rose at the hem. Orrin couldn't jitterbug but he waltzed. Blue Hawaii was the theme. You crossed a bridge over sparkling fake water as you came in and there were plywood palms and a crescent moon. The dance band had come over from Manitou.

I dwell on this prom because though we felt happy we were also wistful since it was a goodbye, to the forties and to our shared life in the schools. Even though most of us would live on there in Earlington, and see each other year in year out, still it was a real goodbye. Officially the dance was seven to eleven but everybody knew it would last till the 11:05 train came through. When we heard the whistle, bright glances said goodbye under the crepe paper streamers. Orrin held my hand as we stood near the bridge watching the dancers.

Each weekday morning Orrin read the Louisville *Courier-Journal* at breakfast. When he looked up at me he was like a schoolteacher grading an essay, when his favorite pupil comes to his desk with a question. He walked to work since it wasn't but three blocks. Some mid-days he came home for lunch (called dinner then), sometimes he'd eat with a client at one of our two cafés on Railroad Street. He was always back by 4:30. We

112

supped at six unless guests were coming, and then it would be 6:30. Our first dinner guest was Mother, who still didn't quite seem to believe I'd made such a good match. I couldn't quite believe it myself. Sometimes it felt like playing grown-up, and so made me feel even younger than I was.

After supper we might take a stroll in good weather, or listen to the radio in the parlor. In the winter it might be snowing, and we'd have coal burning on the grate in the shallow fireplace. We sat like a pair of dolls in our two rockers and listened to the radio or I read Orrin *Forever Amber*, that had people clucking then, though nowadays. . . . I never did get my diploma but I've always been inclined to read when I had time. I don't think Orrin really cared much about the novels—sometimes he dozed off, and he never could remember who was in love with who. I think he just wanted to hear my voice, without having to talk himself.

We walked to church Sundays, prayer meeting Wednesday evenings, and to the picture show some Saturday evenings. We had three vacations. One spring we drove to Oklahoma, where Orrin's sister and her husband ran a motel. Another spring we took Mother to see New Orleans with us. The last vacation was the best. In the winter of '52 we drove to a place that sounded to me like something out of a fairy tale, Daytona Beach, Florida. We spread a towel on the hot sand and sat with the ocean in front of us. Everybody must know we're new, I thought, because of our color. Orrin especially looked white on his back and feet because of the blackness of his chest and the darkness of his legs. But maybe, I thought, they'll think we live here but just don't tan. How do you like the ocean, Orrin wanted to know, after we'd played in it and were back up at our towel. I said I liked the taste of it but give me Earlington Lake for swimming any day.

By then I was starting to wonder why no children had come along. I guess everybody was wondering, but in those days you didn't talk to people's face about such things. Once Mother did go so far as to say she hoped to see some grandchildren before she died. I said well Mother if you weren't so healthy we'd have to start a family sooner. And see if Eddy doesn't show up one of these days with a wife and ten grandchildren for you.

But in truth Orrin hadn't worn condoms for a year. We were down to once a week or so by then but still it seemed we should be having some results. Nowadays a couple would talk about it and maybe see a doctor, but back then it only made us work harder in bed. I remember thinking I wanted to open myself until Orrin would be able to put not just his tommy but all the rest of him too inside me, like I wanted to swallow him down there so he could go far enough back in for the seed not to die again. I kicked him on the back with my heels, Orrin, Orrin. You'd think (though I haven't asked anyone or read anything about this) that the act of love would shrink or blur the rest of the world. For me though it's actually been the reverse, or partly. I mean that while most of the day I wasn't conscious of much more than the room I was working in, love-making stretched my awareness to the whole house, and out up and down the street, the other houses and sometimes farther, I could feel the presence out there of all Earlington and sometimes the surrounding country, and other towns out the roads and railroad tracks.

I expect our life would have gone on in its regular way, me happy to be a premature matron in that narrow deep house with its dank front yard and back yard rising in three modest terraces up to the shed—I had some petunias and glads there, and even a potted japonica under glass—and it would have been a good life too, if Orrin hadn't suddenly died.

It was November, a Tuesday I believe. His law partner was in a neighboring town for the day, and by chance the secretary was on vacation. Orrin was to be home for lunch. When he was late I telephoned the office (no answer) and then got through to Mabel on the ground floor, and got her to send up the stockboy. He found Orrin in the stairwell where he'd evidently been sitting since the heart attack struck him that morning. It must have been like a seizure, he must have felt its aura around him and thought so this is where it ends, and turned around in the echoing well and sat down as the attack hit him. He thought of me, and of twenty other people in passing, as his heart burned and the rest of him felt the coolness coming.

It was a large funeral, with half of Earlington and inlaws from out of state. The will was in order of course, with the estate to me except for token bequests to his family rigorously apportioned according to genealogical distance. People probably thought I'd been left more than I really had. After the funeral and burial and other death expenses I had the house, a few hundred dollars in government bonds and four thousand 1952 dollars in our savings account.

I miss Orrin still. He was reticent, kind and always honorable, with me and with everyone else so far as I've ever known. Now and then I can envision what might be happening to some people after they've died, what they might be doing. Orrin sits outdoors in a spirit Switzerland, on a piazza at a little table under a parasol, reading a spirit *Courier-Journal* about wars and progress among the living, and looking up to watch sailboats out on the lake. A waiter brings him coffee when he needs it.

I didn't go into a formal mourning but I did seem to enter a kind of suspended animation. It was a long winter. I seemed always to be in the kitchen stocking the old wood-burning cookstove, scratching embroidery and initials in the frost flowers on the windowpane. It was an informal mourning. The town recognized it and people were good, and no man

114

who knew me would have thought of paying me court in the first year of my widowhood. I seemed to have inherited silence and maybe loneliness too, that cold winter.

One April weekend I decided it was time to bestir myself. Southern Bell was hiring and I thought I could say number please, so Monday morning I went for an interview at the new office. Who knows why, but I'd dolled myself up in navy dotted Swiss, navy and white pumps and my straw with cherries, with a cherry red Cupid's bow I knew was outdated. The interviewer, a classmate's mother, practically assured me of the job. If this didn't work out I had an application in for receptionist at the Pepsi bottling plant over in Nebo. I was feeling good.

Some of the forsythia around the parking lot was blooming. The lot was bright and empty. My dark green Chevvy, only five years old, parked as near the door of the stucco building as possible, for the first time ever looked like something Goofy in the comics might drive, it was so high and rounded.

To make a long story short, a lineman helped me when my car didn't crank. He raised the green hood and fixed it. He had grey-white hair, he was twenty-nine, slight but with a terribly solicitous manner in flat brown eyes and in the whispery voice that came out his wide mouth, a whispery voice that carried more authority than I was accustomed to, and tiny muscles that flinched under his eyes.

"You made it look so easy," I said. "I don't know how I can thank you."

"I'm Monte, Monte Kercheval. You can let me take you to the picture show tonight over in Madisonville. I already saw what they have here."

"So did I, Monte," I lied. Birds hopped over the asphalt like dust bunnies in the breeze. "I'm Maggie Utley."

Later I learned he'd borrowed the car he picked me up in that evening from a fellow lineman. Over in Madisonville nobody knew me. It was ten miles away and had grown faster than Earlington. At the pictures and then at the café for pie I felt conscious of the luxury of anonymity for the first time.

"I'm a drifter, Maggie." Monte was renting an apartment over the hardware store on Railroad Street in Earlington, had transferred from Southern Bell in Henderson, had been with the phone company two years and before that worked any number of jobs in southern Indiana and western Kentucky. I remember he was wearing a charcoal silk cowboy shirt with pink piping at the collar and pockets. He exhaled his cigarette smoke in a sigh through pursed lips. He wanted to have his own auto body shop some day. I said, "You should do that. You'll get yourself electrocuted if you keep climbing those telephone poles, Monte."

By the time we got back the whole street was dark. A neighbor or two

115

might have slipped up a venetian blind slat to look, but my front porch was sheltered with wisteria in the latticework. Monte asked when he could see me again and then he asked if he could kiss me good night. It was a kind of kiss I'd never had. His wide mouth was partly opened and his tongue moved back and forth over my lips. I circled him lightly with my arms, and felt his ribs under the silk, and I ran my fingers through his cornsilky mop of hair.

Once I told Monte, "You're like my brother Eddy."

The corners of his lips moved back in that soundless half-smile of his. He paused. "Did Eddy like the Sons of the Pioneers too?" By then we were making love often in his shabby apartment in the middle of the night with radio music on, it made my head swim.

"I mean about leaving your folks back in Cairo, not writing."

"Listen, Mag. I paid them what I owed before I left, working my tail off and. . . . And anyway they've all left Cairo, without a forwarding address." I didn't know whether he was hypothesizing, or telling simple truth, or lying outright. It was often that way with Monte.

We talked like that after love in his bed over the hardware store. I saw he wasn't going to bring up the subject of marriage so after a while I asked him what he might think of the idea. Monte pressed his lips together. He got up and pulled on his slacks. Still without a word he went barefoot and bare-chested like a famine victim over to the table by the window. Sometimes Monte seemed to be playing a part in a movie in his mind, with closeups and soughing violins. He shook a Lucky out of the pack and lighted it with a match rasped under the table. In the wash from the streetlight his naked flat nipples were almost as pale as his skin. His Adam's apple bobbed before he spoke. "We'd have to leave Earlington."

A chill went through me. The fan on the table turned its face back and forth, pulling some of the night air in through the screenwire, diffusing Monte's cigarette smoke in it. I tugged at the corner of a pillow.

Monte said, "We could go to a city. Living in a city is like traveling even when you stay there." He hadn't looked my way and he still didn't as he sucked on his cigarette. He blew out the smoke. "I'm liable to run out on you after fifteen months, Mag. Down where it counts I'm no good. I'm not worth the trouble."

I said, "Yes you are. Your ribs are worth the trouble."

His white voice darkened and roughened in the back of his mouth. "Let's tie the knot then. First time for me, I didn't expect it ever to happen. Let's sell your house and move to Louisville. I'll breathe freer."

"You're on," I said, though privately I was giving myself a fortnight to think it over. I'd never lived anywhere but Earlington. And then there was the question of how it would look. Still less than a year's widow, swept off my feet by someone as rootless as Monte Kercheval? I didn't want to embarrass Mother.

In the end we married secretly and Monte went ahead to Louisville to find us a house. I took the Southern Bell job, worked at it for a few months and arranged to be transferred. Jim and Lucy Teague, she a classmate, bought my house.

Louisville seemed vast. We lived in an aimless neighborhood in the west end not far from the river, a neighborhood that never stopped feeling like a tent city all the time I was there. Peeling paint and weedy lawns, dogs, small nondescript enterprises like Monte's Body Shop eleven blocks west on a different street (from one end of Earlington to another it wasn't eleven blocks). I'd stored my old furniture at Mother's and when I saw the Louisville house and neighborhood, and how Monte would be looking every day when he came home from work, I decided to furnish the place out of thrift stores. There wasn't time for proper housework anyway, with me working forty hours at Bell. As the body shop established itself it became more dependable, but it never was any great success. Monte had a series of teenagers as part-time helpers, and later a full-time employee. At the pound we got a pup that looked to be wirehair and rat terrier and named him Bill. He lived at the shop to keep Monte company and to be a watchdog at night. Monte liked most any kind of animal, and said he wanted to live in the country some day and have a goat.

But Monte didn't want any children. At first we couldn't afford it (though you only had to look around to see that people always manage to afford children). Later the reasons changed, or there were none. I remember one Sunday in May or June around 1960, I was in my late twenties. We'd had a quarrel that morning about something—we never went to church, Monte hated churches. We'd sulked through lunch with an extra beer apiece (he drank beer like water, was accustoming me to it, though I drew the line at whiskey). To give ourselves a chance to make up we drove over for a walk in Fontaine Ferry Park (people called it Fountain Ferry, it's gone now). Broody and silent we heard music and followed a gravel walk toward it, around a white lilac and there was the carrousel turning with gleaming children astride the effigies. I shivered and said the children were beautiful. I turned to Monte, thinking only that the sight must have moved him too, and so would have reconciled us.

He had paled—it was as if the air had darkened abound his face. And it was as if the lilac blossoms had shared his dismay. Fast as I could I said, "It wasn't a rebuke, I was just talking. I wasn't thinking about us." Monte searched me and believed me, inhaled and laughed his soundless laugh.

117

I could hear the carrousel again as color came back into his face and we walked past the lilac.

By then I was working first shift at the phone company. It had taken me seven years to come up from graveyard through night. Hattie Rattigan's locker was next to mine—we came about the same time and were promoted more or less together. We never saw the inside of each other's houses but in the employee lounge over in a corner we'd munch Nabs and sip Nehi and confide in an oblique way, give each other glimpses of fairly sizeable tracts of our private lives. She was ten years older, a divorced mother of two. From the beginning we were both long distance. There was another room for information (directory assistance now) and a third, the biggest, for local operators, which changed function as Louisville switched to dial.

After a while Hattie and I had adjacent switchboard stations. There we'd sit in our headsets two hours at a stretch answering signals for calls to anywhere (all over the country, Canada and Europe and other parts of the world from time to time, Australia, you name it—once I had one to Tunisia that didn't get through), and between calls we could talk there too.

Eventually I had to let Mother know about Monte. The only proper cleaning the house had was for her 1964 visit. Even clean it made her face fall but she shrugged and came to terms. She and Monte seemed to like each other, out of a wary respect. But the absence of children needed explanation and none I gave was adequate, I could see. I didn't manage to tell her the truth, that I'd come to suspect one of us was infertile. We were using pills by then and I'd secretly stopped taking them, with no result yet. Mother stayed a week and caught me up on Earlington news. She'd had a postcard from Eddy two years before, from Oregon without return address. There was no longer passenger train service between Earlington and Louisville, so Mother traveled Greyhound. "Next time we'll come for you," I told her as she boarded for the night trip back.

For a year I'd known Monte had a girlfriend, from her perfume I could sometimes smell on his neck. She was a waitress in a fishhouse out near Bellarmine College, a divorcee. It came to a head when she needed an abortion and talked Monte into paying for it, the trip to Mexico and all. He told me what the money was going for at breakfast, in his resigned way that brooked no reproach. Not that I had any to give, or only that he was too old for those carryings-on, but I held my tongue, he looked so fragile and shrunken.

Mother had a stroke, went into a rest home and died. Something told me not to sell the house so I found renters. Monte's death the same fall wasn't nearly so easy. Lung cancer from the years of cigarettes took its time with him. I saw him die, gasping and trying to speak under an oxygen tent. I said "Don't try to talk. It's nearly over." The thin sheet was almost more than his poor rib cage could bear. I remember his frightened eyes, pleading. There was nothing I could do. The end came like a darkness seeping from the edges of his field of vision in toward my face. I forgive him what there is to forgive, and I miss him. Now he coasts over western Kentucky and southern Indiana, over the drive-ins, Kentucky Dam, over the telephone poles and auto graveyards. His pale silky hair lifts, as if the night were moving her own fingers through it.

It took a good two years to wind up the sale of the shop and house. I moved into an apartment near the art museum. Most of the people in the building were retired but I continued to work at Bell. So through the turbulent sixties I lived more quietly and monotonously than ever before, going to the odd movie with Hattie from work, reading novels and biographies. I came to enjoy living alone and having so much time to myself. In my late thirties I still had occasional invitations to dinner or whatever from men at work, and other operators offered to fix me up with blind dates, but I always made up an excuse to say no. People said I must have a secret boyfriend.

In 1971 on my thirty-eighth birthday I decided to try to turn forty back in Earlington. I put in my transfer request the next week and by a fluke word came that a position would open in six months. I thought I should jump at the chance since Earlington hadn't grown any in the last ten years, so I gave the rentors notice to vacate and in November I moved back to the house I was born and raised in.

Three-quarters of the people on the street had never lived elsewhere. They welcomed me back, my return one more testimonial to the wisdom of their ways. But it was a true small-town welcome, not what I'd foolishly let myself dream in Louisville. They didn't open hearts and homes for the sake of old times. They were helpful and friendly but they needed no intimacy with me, and were incurious about my life away from Earlington. And as they saw I wasn't going to accept invitations to church, prayer meeting, sewing circle, they cooled and drew back, still amiably.

I'd been there some two years and settled into an easy routine, day shift with Friday and Saturday off, meals cooked on the new gas range, meals more and more like abridgements of Mother's wood-stove ones. I was watching the cold late December early dark settle into the back yard. Some lights were on through the house but no curtains were drawn yet, and I heard the old doorbell being turned. When I switched on the weak porch light, through the etched glass I saw a large bearded man in an overcoat and a wide-brim hat.

I opened the door and said "Yes?" and then seemed to fall through several depths of understanding as he said, "Maggie, you're the spit and image of mother. My knees are jelly."

119

Eddy my brother. Behind him at the curb stood a ten-year-old black Cadillac with a silver Airstream trailer behind it. "Eddy." Searching, doubting and wondering, falling into each other's arms.

He had a good wife, Rae, and a girl and three boys. It seemed they lived most of the year in New Mexico and the rest on the road wholesaling turquoise and copper jewelry. They stayed a week in Earlington, laid wreaths on Mother's and Poppa's graves, and heard about my life up to then.

One morning while Rae took the children to Madisonville to see Santa at a shopping mall Eddy had a chance to fill me in on his life. When he first left home he'd done farmwork for a few years in the midwest, but never made or kept enough for him to feel like coming back to see us. And then he'd wandered into a life of honky-tonks and petty crime, and been captured in an armed robbery at a gas station near St. Louis. And so he spent six years in the penitentiary, years he didn't want to say much about.

Eddy'd been paroled in 1961 and lived twelve years in Kansas City, Missouri, and St. Joseph working days as a furniture mover and evenings and Saturdays as an auctioneer. He and Rae met on the circuit—she was an auctioneer too. When she was pregnant she told Eddy she aimed to have the baby, she could raise it without any help from him and he was under no obligation. But Eddy said that when he first held that warm little bundle he decided to propose. Rae's half Apache, born in Arizona, and it was her idea for them to move out there. Eddy said he'd thought Mother and Poppa might be gone by now, and he'd feared never to find me. He said not to worry about his share of my house.

We opened presents and ate Christmas dinner together before they had to start back to Santa Fe. They left on a snowy morning, the children giggling and boxing. "You come to see us," Rae said when she hugged me goodbye. I told Eddy to keep in touch. "Goodbye Aunt Maggie," the children screamed when the car started. "Goodbye, goodbye, goodbye," snowflakes melting against my face.

I was forty when I waved goodbye to Eddy and his family. My life quietened for some eighteen months, and I enjoyed it well enough until somebody mentioned the month I had coming and I realized I'd simply forgotten to take a vacation in the past year. I decided it was time for me to have some kind of fling, do something peculiar.

Browsing one Saturday through the classifieds of a free weekly from the A&P I saw an ad for macramé lessons. Okay, I thought, let's give it a whirl. I didn't even know what macramé was—a martial art? A woman answered at the Madisonville number. Yes, a beginner's class would begin Monday evening. Once a week, two dollars a two-hour lesson plus materials. All I needed bring to the first meeting was the desire.

The address was in a new subdivision on the near edge of Madisonville, in a cluster of townhouse apartments. By Monday night I knew what macramé was and was prepared for the odor of jute and hemp that filled the stairwell when Hilda Ruby opened her door. I'll always associate that circus odor with the young man in a Hawaiian shirt and cut-off jeans my classmate and I met at the entry door later that evening after the lesson. My classmate said, "You don't have a daughter looking for a husband do you? He's a bachelor, a Smoot with some funny first name."

Next Monday night my classmate couldn't attend because her husband had a wisdom tooth out. I learned six new knots and how to incorporate clay beads and twigs. I was careful to leave at the same time, or slightly earlier. The week before, young Mr. Smoot's smile had crossed my class-mate and come to rest on me with an inquisitiveness that had nothing to do with daughters. I was sure he would be there in the stairwell or outside with his curls and palm trees, but it took two more Mondays.

Lysander (people would complain, "Lysandra, that sounds like a woman's name"—I called him Ly) lived above my teacher Hilda. He was twenty-eight, thin and pretty with his bushy moustache and brown curls. There was I, forty-one, thinking "Shame, Margaret, shame!" as I lost my classmate, feigned to return for advice about my macramé project, feigned indecision as he mounted the stairs with his shirttails flapping. "You look lost," he said.

I explained that I was making up my mind not to disturb Hilda. And then, marveling at my boldness, I said, "How's the weather? She promised to show us the view from her balcony but she never opened the drapes."

"Her view can't be as good as mine." From that interchange it was like clockwork, like in the movies, so predictable that one could be very graceful about it through that evening and night and the next morning. The old story, except for the ages and the sexes (the old story with one beginning and twenty middles and three or four endings).

Ly taught cosmetology at the beauty college that had opened in the old feed store behind the Earlington Post Office. I said, "I thought you were all homosexual."

"Some are," he said. His six students at the time were all female and young, none anywhere close to repellent, and all could have sued him for sexual harassment if they hadn't been the harassers and he the compliant victim. "Hairdressers more than cosmetologists for some reason, it seems." He tugged my earlobe. A big summer moon shone through the open screenwire. "But don't go jumping to conclusions with nobody, Ma'am. What time should I set the alarm for?" I slept like a baby.

Where did you learn your tricks, Lysander? Flowers, picnics, strolls under that autumn's Perseids. He was a winning lanky charmer for sure, wreathed in chestnut curls, the first man with a moustache I'd ever kissed. Several things I expected to happen didn't. He didn't ask for money, and he didn't offer helpful suggestions about my appearance either. Finally I asked him if I should do my face differently. "Who knows? But don't change too much right away." And neither of us decided to call a halt. I was feeling lighter and naughtier by the week, and happier, and coming to love this Lysander Smoot. Increasingly he shrugged off the attentions of his students. With me—and he was with me more and more of our free time—he was ever more affectionate, and I was content to let it go on as long as it would. One thing I didn't at all expect to happen did.

According to records I had, Poppa's family had been in western Kentucky since before the civil war (Mother's ancestry was in Appalachia and untraceable). And there was supposed to be a family cemetery somewhere between Cadiz and Gracey. Saturdays, our common days off, Ly and I looked for it and finally found it in a grove surrounded by fallow cropland. A grocer at a crossroads had said an old woman down the road ought to know where it was. She came to her door with a shotgun—there had been a robbery in the area a week before—and told us where the cemetery ought to be, a few miles away. "It ain't but ten graves or so," she warned, leaning on her shotgun.

In the dun airy copse we found the untended graveyard, every stone for a Rideout, the most recent from a generation ago. I felt Ly's hands on my shoulders, his front against my back. "Will you marry me?" he said.

It took me a long time to reply. I listened to the birds singing and didn't turn around. Why should he want marriage? What would people say? Then I turned, for us to see and judge each other clearly. I told him how little I'd expected this, and said I failed to see the point since as we were we seemed happier than ordinary humans had any right to be. He listened as if I were a child providing circumstantial detail in a narrative whose conclusion alone mattered. But if he was sure it was what he wanted, I said, then my answer was yes a hundred times. A fortnight later before the justice of the peace I couldn't help loving telling myself, "Shame, Margaret, shame!"

Heard you got married again, Mag, people would say. Tongues may have wagged behind my back, but to my face that light "again" was as far as the criticism went. It would have gone farther had our walls been transparent. We didn't always make love in bed or at night. We didn't wear any nightwear to bed. Nobody does any more, Ly said. I enjoyed sleeping naked and didn't see anything wrong with it, but for the sake of appearances I purchased pajamas for us both at the Railroad Street Penny's.

I wish him well. In the year of our marriage I think I laughed more than ever before in my life. I remember one Saturday in the end of winter we drove out into the country and walked in the snow-covered fields. My smoky breath made me say I was a dragon whereupon Ly picked up a length of branch for a pike and said he was Saint George. I smiled, shaking my head but he said run, dragon, better run. His horse pawed the earth and neighed. I ran shrieking and laughing over the snow until I stumbled and fell, and Saint George was on me covering my face with kisses, and I thought my heart would break from happiness.

Contraception wasn't a problem since I'd had menopause the year before. We talked some about adopting a child but Ly wasn't really interested. I hesitate to say what did come to interest him that spring: establishing his own beauty college. They think they know (he would say of his colleagues and bosses) but they're only talking fashion. Beauty is something else and ought to be taught, and people aren't fools — can you imagine Earlington the Mecca of beauty? When he went out on that limb I wondered if our marriage too weren't never-never stuff.

Then, unexpectedly as the proposal, came the announcement of his intention to go to Spain and his request for a divorce. He'd always love me and miss me, but he'd discovered he had to have his freedom. Immediately I thought, now's the shame, Margaret, now comes when you'll want to hide. I asked him why but I knew there'd be no real answer for that. I asked him what he planned to do in Spain. See the country, learn the language. Why, why — but there was no point in asking, he may not have known why himself. And he was of an age (and a sex) when one is susceptible to adventure.

We split the cost of the divorce and he left with no more money than he'd brought into the marriage. Better off without him, people offered, more fish in the sea. He's sent me postcards now and again over the past seven years, none from Spain but from Seattle, Alaska and Japan (did he learn that language?). I wish Ly well and when he dies I wish him an apartment to his liking and a beauty college with his name on it.

I still live in the house I was born in, working at Bell, cooking for myself alone again, reading, taking awkward vacations. I never cared enough about macramé to take the intermediate class but the other day I was thinking about it and it occurred to me that I'd made a kind of design in my life with the one knot of marriage. I'm fifty, fifteen years to retirement. Last year I went out to New Mexico on my vacation to see Eddy and Rae and their nearly grown children. Earlington with its strange integrity will be engulfed by its growing neighbor. I'll live on here and watch the changes. When I'm gone, lay Margaret Rideout Utley Kercheval Smoot's body in that wet old Earlington cemetery, next to Poppa and Mother. I'll stay home upstairs at a window, and watch the cars and pedestrians through the years and wish them well.

YOURS

Y O U   R E M E M B E R   W E used to talk about traveling in Kentucky and seeing my father's birthplace. I was in the mountains and I've been here in Bardstown for a week. The hotel is 130 years old and parts of the town are beautiful.

Today for breakfast I walked to a café in the business district: worn linoleum, a juke box, "Vera" and "Connie" according to their badges, the establishment's first dollar framed between an inspection certificate and "If you're so Smart/Why aren't you *Rich?*" in faded Day-Glow green. Feisty little Vera game me an inquisitive smile. I'm off newspapers for the moment and to fill the breakfast time this morning I plotted a graph of my life on a napkin. The eight or nine other customers had pegged me for a tourist. A plumber and a shopkeeper were arguing placidly about cars. The day was beginning.

I spent some time in the local bookstore, alone except for the proprietress. There was a good supply of biography and children's but otherwise the supply was freakish. I finally bought a paperback Agatha Christie I didn't think I'd read, a heavy and expensive *Architectural Heritage of Kentucky* and our favorite film star's autobiography. Then I walked. Spring comes more deliberately here and the streets are almost deserted. I carried my books in a shopping bag with handles.

Gravitating toward houses that were old but not renovated, I walked through poorer and poorer neighborhoods into a black district at one edge of town. Older women taking the sun on their porches watched me with curiosity. In the doorway of a grocery stood a short stocky fellow around thirty. As I came near he asked me how I was doing. He said, "You're not from here, are you?" He had been married but his wife had died, he lived in a pair of rooms behind the store. "What kind of living do you make?" I said. "Do you want to get married again?" He said it was the onliest thing he looked forward to. I said, "Listen, I'd like you to have one of these books here." He chose the one with pictures of mansions. "Good luck," I said. He said, "The very same to you."

In five minutes I was in rolling pastureland with occasional ponds and clumps of trees. I just kept walking away from town, climbing fences and giving wide berth to the grazing cattle, happy not to see anyone for a couple of hours until I came to the navel of the universe, the Platonic idea of the farmhouse with dust and a yellow dog, thoughtful hens under the hydrangea, wads of cotton stuck in the screen door to discourage flies. "Hoo-oo," I called. The breeze had risen, white clouds were piled high in the blue sky, wash flapped on the line.

"My, who's that?" Peering and smiling the mistress of the house appeared, tall as I am and heavier, around sixty and laughing at my city clothes and sunburn. "Are you lost?" She had a twinkling direct smile like a nun's. I asked for a drink of water. "Yes, yes, come in. Do you have time?" Inside it was cool and smelled of lavender. "I'm Katie Sisk, everybody calls me Katie," she said. I sat in the small dining room and she brought a pitcher of ice water and then potato salad and ham sandwiches and lemon meringue pie. I told Katie what I'd left, where I'd been, how when I'd begun wandering or fleeing I'd seemed to be reborn. She said, "Well goodness gracious," smiling and shaking her head without a hint of approval or disapproval. After a while we worked into an odd sort of a conversation: she was crocheting, I was sipping coffee, I would ask almost any question that popped into my head, she'd reply and then there would be silence until I thought of something else to ask.

"Did you always live around here, Katie?"

"I was born in this house."

"Did you ever have a serious illness?"

"I go to bed soon after dark and I'm up before sunrise. Now and again I might have a touch of the rheumatism."

"Ever been to a quilting bee?"

"More than I can remember. I'm surprised you know what they are."

"What do you think of me, Katie?"

"What kind of a question is that? Heavens."

"Are you ever gloomy?"

"Goodness!"

"Katie, I have two books here in my shopping bag. I'd like you to have one."

"No, there wouldn't be any point. My eyes aren't so keen as they used

125

to be, and then I never did do much reading. I'll give you a ride back to town though, if that's where you're going. I have some shopping to do."

I rode beside her in her pickup truck and when she let me off she said, "Stay out of trouble."

It was 3:30 and I was tired enough for a nap and yet something inclined me to prolong the afternoon. In the window of a place called "Curios and Antiques" some depression glass table settings of a sort I remembered from childhood caught my eye. Inside the store even I could tell that the merchandise was mostly worthless gimcrackery. That and the clutter pleased me, and the fact that I had to scan the place several times before I saw the owner sitting in the rear, an etiolated Mark Twain gussied up with fly-away hair and string tie but thin and wan, immobile as a turtle on a log, watching me.

He smiled and nodded. At first he left me to wander on my own but soon he began, still sitting where he was, to comment on whatever I happened to be looking at. I was noncommital but I must have seemed an easy mark because he warmed to his task, feeling me out by quoting prices — at first reasonably unreasonable ones and then, when I showed no dismay, more and more outrageous ones, fluttering his eyelids and caressing the junk. His energy and cunning entranced me. "Wasn't there something," he asked, "something in the window you were noticing from the street?"

"Yes," I said. "The green glass tableware."

"I should have guessed. Ravishing, isn't it?"

"Yes," I said, "it is."

"Yes, yes, Czechoslovak, you know. Eighteenth century. Very rare."

I felt giddy. "They're well preserved."

"Aren't they. The family that . . . but I'm not at liberty to disclose the story."

"I see. And about the price?"

He spoke in an undertone behind his hand. "I had them appraised last month and he said two five for the set. But you obviously appreciate them, so I could arrange a discount. I'd hate them to go to someone who. . . ."

"I wonder if I could sleep on it," I said. "I don't like to ask you to hold them, though."

"Not at all."

"I'll try to stop in tomorrow then. Oh, and by the way, I bought some books this morning and then discovered I won't have time to read them. I'd like you to have one."

He pounced on the autobiography. "I've literally been dying to read this. Could I? Just to borrow?" As I left he laid his hand on my arm. "I hope you won't let yourself be put off by . . . by these people." He gestured toward the world outside his shop. "They do have their little points."

Returning to the hotel I amost danced. I slept, showered, and went down to dine in the hotel restaurant. Sometimes I think differences in restaurants' bills of fare shrink to insignificance compared to differences in ambience. Food's food but place is all there is. This one still has up its Christmas decorations and there's a mural of the region's history beginning with Indians and culminating in this hotel. A candle floated in a brandy snifter on my table. There were no conversations near enough for eavesdropping, and so I cogitated.

It was then that I thought about you and wondered why I shouldn't love your small-mindedness after all. Surprised? I often have surprising revelations lately. In fact it was they that first made me suspect I had suffered rebirth—the revelations that showered over me in the little train chugging down through the crazy towns, as with every mile more of you and the rest of my life was torn from my mind. Dining slowly I remembered that train ride only three months ago through the snowy night, the various stations at any of which I might have alighted, and finally the next day the station from which I telephoned to say I was off to seek my fortune and would not be back.

After a mint julep pie and coffee I took another walk, up back streets, across a gas station parking lot under a full moon with dogs barking, new leaves moving on the trees and the stars I remember from childhood shining down through the clear air. It seemed that only our treading would keep the earth turning. A policeman in his patrol car asked, "What'cha up to, friend?" There were a few fireflies even this early in the spring. The public library was closing as I passed.

It was 9:30 and I came back to the hotel. Quiet laughter and music drew me to the bar where I settled back into a red Naugahyde booth with a cognac in the dark. Eight or nine other people were there and as I watched them and heard scraps of their conversation it occurred to me that this was a cast party celebrating a run that had lasted fifty years for some of them already.

An attractive dark-haired girl came in alone, I invited her to join me and to my surprise she did. She was Alice, in her early twenties with white skin, large eyes and a wide unsmiling mouth, living in the hotel until she found an apartment. She'd come from Mississippi to be assistant buyer in a clothing store. I sketched my history and recent travels and she asked where I planned to go next. I said I hadn't thought about it. Half closing here eyes she said she'd have gone to New York except that her father didn't want her to be so far away. Her father is called Beau because he was so handsome. Alice's favorite color is orange, but violet looks better on her. She said she eats onion sandwiches, "Just bread and mayon-

127

naise and lots of onion. They give me headaches but I eat them anyway."
And then unexpectedly she said, "I have to go now," laying her white
hand on mine.

"Alice," I protested.

"Really, I can't."

The Agatha Christie was in my pocket and so I took it out and gave it
to her. "I bought it this morning but I don't think I'll get around to
reading it."

She smiled for the first time and then bent down and kissed me on the
cheek. Yes, I was disappointed, but if I stay on here something more
might happen tomorrow or the next day.

After Alice had gone I sat in the bar for an hour longer remembering
the day. The black grocer, Katie the farm woman, the antique dealer and
Alice from Mississippi all in one day, a pretty good average. Toying with
that fact must have prompted a fantasy of an old and intricate lodge
somewhere in wooded mountains where they and I could all be together
for weeks at a time, all each other's disciples as we wandered the long
hallways or gathered at night around the fire. Why isn't there such a
place anyway? when clearly there ought to be. There are fewer things in
heaven and earth than are dreamt of in my philosophy.

It was after eleven when I came up to my room. I remembered you
again, and decided to write this letter. Not that I suppose I owe it: it's a
gift. And so I've sat down at my desk and filled up these pages, saying
quite a bit less about you than I'd expected to. I'm sorry. I'll be gone from
here by the time this reaches you. I doubt that we'll ever see one another
again. If we do, we won't be recognizable. Still and all I remain, with
love, sincerely yours.

ABOUT THE AUTHOR

Joe Ashby Porter, born and raised in Kentucky, teaches at Duke University and has directed the Duke University Writers' Conference as well as the Jesse Stuart Creative Writing Workshop in Kentucky. He is the author of *Eelgrass,* a novel, and has had stories published in a number of distinguished magazines and anthologies, including *New Directions in Prose and Poetry,* the *Pushcart Prize,* and *Best American Short Stories.* In addition, he has served as fiction editor of the magazine *Crazyhorse* and, as Joseph A. Porter, is author of *The Drama of Speech Acts,* a study of four Shakespearean plays.

The Johns Hopkins University Press

THE KENTUCKY STORIES

*This book was composed in Palatino text type
by David Lorton and Caslon Openface by the
Composing Room from a design by Susan
P. Fillion. It was printed on S. D. Warren's
50-lb. Sebago Eggshell Cream paper and bound in
Holliston Sturdetan by Universal Lithographer's, Inc.*